A WEB OF SALVAGE

I went through the wheelhouse door like an express train, grabbing for the telegraph. We needed power now, all the thrust we could get to dodge that prowling freighter out there. Because somehow I knew that, while the *Sarikamis* was struggling to increase momentum, we were to be her next target.

There was insanity in that storm-lashed bay off the North African coast, and in the next three or four minutes I was going to have to play a freakish game of tip and run with an eight thousand ton avalanche of steel, suddenly run amok . . .

BRIAN CALLISON

A Web
of Salvage

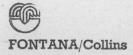

FONTANA/Collins

First published by William Collins 1973
First issued in Fontana Books 1975

© Brian Callison 1973

Made and printed in Great Britain by
William Collins Sons & Co Ltd Glasgow

CHAPTER ONE

She was dying.

And, now it had come, she would die very quickly indeed.

We even knew how it would happen. She would capsize. We sensed it the moment that last over-stressed bulkhead started to scream. Just before the scream converted to the muted thunder of whirlpooling cargo and buckling metal as the sea cataracted into number three lower hold, while the ship herself – or what there was left of her after the collision – shook sullenly, sort of lifting her head for a last brief moment as if still trying to die with a little pride left.

And then lay over in a tired, almost apologetic gesture of submission.

Tanker said 'Bugger it!' and began to inflate his Beaufort Jacket with long, deliberate breaths, as if we had all the time in the world to get clear.

Except that we hadn't. You never do. Not when a half-ship can't fight any more.

I still tried to make the signal, though. Running for the Very pistol lying ready loaded on the chart-room table, just as the first roaring water smashed in over the starboard bulwarks and snatched Nicholson clean off the centrecastle ladder leaving only a thin, utterly disbelieving shriek suspended over the bedlam to prove he'd ever been with us at all.

I didn't stop running until the deck became an impossible uphill scramble, while the open chart-room door ceased to be a destination and turned inexorably into a gaping roof over my head instead. Then I suddenly remembered that my lifejacket was on the table beside the Very pistol and reflected irrelevantly, 'The Dragon's got you f'r bloody sure this time, Mister . . .

Which was a pretty silly thing to think about, really. But so was our being on board this particular derelict in the first place, for that matter. Especially when we'd all realised, long before we'd ever set foot on her already sloping decks, that she didn't have the chance of a drowned sailorman of staying afloat.

Her own master had certainly known. He'd abandoned her the night before we arrived.

But maybe, even though he was condemning his own ship, he still wasn't quite as desperate as we were to save that insignificant little hulk.

Maybe, for him, her going didn't mean the end of a very precious dream.

The dream had started six years ago for John and I. It was a dream of gladiators and dragons, and battles where every seafaring cloud held a promise of sharing in its silver lining, and where every seaborne plea for help held out, under all the fear and suffering, our open invitation to joust in the biggest arena in the world. Except that in our dream the maidens in distress were the crippled ships, and the Ocean was our particular Dragon.

And we were the gladiators, John and I. Along with Tanker the Bosun, and Nicholson the deckhand and all the others in our crew. Together we rode towards our Dragon like any Knights of yore — only our steed was a two hundred and twenty foot tug called *Tactician*, and instead of the Maiden's favours we were seeking a rather more tangible reward.

The dream fades a little when the Knight's purse is empty and he's in need of yet another load of bunker fuel, or wages for the varlets, or stores or tools, or towing gear, or a replacement liferaft because the last one blew to shreds under a force ten breath from the Dragon.

It becomes a nightmare then. You start taking chances and

ignoring the odds. You risk your life in trying to save ships which already have the mark of death plain in their shattered hulls.

It's the time when the ocean salvage game will kill you.

When you become desperate. Like we we were, by then.

As the part-ship started to roll I remember reflecting on how odd it is that you still want to hang on to something, even when your world's pivoting upside down and you know that if you stay you're gripping a three thousand ton sinker.

I'd suddenly found that, instead of standing on the bridge wing I was actually lying along it, and instead of looking through the wheelhouse I was now gazing in close-up at the cracked, broken seams of the planking while brooding vaguely, 'That'll need picking out and re-caulking to stay watertight . . .' Then I craned my head upwards, staring past my hands with the knuckles white as they clawed at the base of the starboard door, and up into the wheelhouse itself with only the grey, storm-tattered clouds on the other side.

I felt the ship going and tried to pretend it wasn't happening at all, concentrating on the chipped green paint of the abandoned telemotor pedestal abaft the soft brassy gleam of the binnacle. Then I frowned critically at the ever canting course board with its irrelevant reminder to a long gone helmsman that the ship's head should be steering zero six eight degrees true . . .

. . . just before he found there wasn't a head to steer to, any more. Or a forepeak, or a number one hold or anything else forward of the cargo-spilling amputation left by the ship which had sliced through her in the night. Some undermanned Liberian tanker which couldn't even ring its engines to full stern for three minutes after the impact. That kind of homicidal juggernaut which sails with two men and a dog as crew — and it's the bloody dog on watch when the auto-pilot fails and the monster runs amok . . .

Tanker yelled sharply, 'You goin' to sleep up there or can

we go now, Skipper!'

I screwed round and felt the shock starting to hit me. She was still capsizing, I could sense the strain on my arms steadily increasing as my full weight came on them, but the roll was slower now, more sluggish, almost as if she hadn't quite surrendered to the forces of equilibrium.

Then something big tore away below – maybe a part of her main engine – and the temporary shift of her righting moment held her almost on her side with the water smashing in great white-streaked fingers along the line of her starboard hatch coamings. I was acutely conscious of the agonised shudders transmitted through her hull though, as each new wave punched into her belly, and I knew it wasn't really a reprieve so much as a prolonging of the death act.

I stared along the deck – *down* the deck – at the Bosun and, just for a moment, couldn't understand why I could see the shiny pink dome of his shaven skull surrounded by the brighter orange halo of the Beaufort Jacket. Then he arched his head back to look up at me and I realised he was still standing vertically, though by now he had one foot on the deck and the other half raised as a prop against the inboard side of the bridge wing.

He said impassively above a lull in the wind, 'Nicholson's gone. Not that it makes much difference.'

It didn't either, under the circumstances – except, maybe, to Nicholson. Or perhaps drowning should be a private thing anyway, and performed without the indignity of an audience of retching fellow shipmates. I still screwed my eyes against the spindrift and scanned along the marching troughs of the waves for a blob of face though. Just in case Nicholson didn't think like me.

I never found out whether he did or not. We didn't see him again. But *Tactician* was out there in that berserk grey Mediterranean dawn too, with Johnny probably prowling round and round in her wheelhouse and waiting grimly for the green Very to tell him we were ready to take the tow – or that red I hadn't quite managed to send to tell him the wreck had decided to kill us instead.

It meant that a minute speck called Harry Nicholson didn't have a chance. There was a whole ocean-going tugboat out there with him – and I couldn't see *her* either.

A breaking sea atomised against the centrecastle below us and Tanker disappeared momentarily in a haze of clouding spray. I thought bitterly, 'Ah, what the hell . . .' and let go, sliding crazily down the streaming planking towards him to bring up against the angled bridge side with a crash.

He spat irritably, then grinned. 'Steady as you go, Skipper. Watch the bloody paintwork.'

It made me feel a lot better. Being beside Tanker again.

'You see the boat anywhere?' I panted.

He didn't grin this time. 'Negative! But *that*'s kind of academic, too. We couldn't make ten yards in this sea . . . five f'r you, of course – seeing how you didn't bother to bring your lifejacket.'

I shrugged. 'So I'm the last of the adventure sailors . . . Maybe we won't have to. Lying off to windward they could float the dinghy down on a line . . . !'

Then something else ripped inside her belly and she sagged even further over until we were standing almost up and down on the bridge side, just leaning rigidly back against the deck and staring hypnotically as a hissing angry sea reached like a black oil blister to just below our feet one moment then, almost as violently, fell away into the trough until we had fifteen feet of vertigo between it and us.

Tanker whispered an involuntary 'Chr*is*t!' and it was the first time I'd ever seen him scared. It was also like looking into a mirror. Then the fear went out of his eyes and the old sardonic defiance came back. He turned his head to face me, unconsciously keeping the back of it pressed hard against the teak planking so the Beaufort billowed up around his ears like an orange pillow.

'Do we stay or go, Skipper? Not that it makes . . .'

The ship shuddered again. The next wave crest slamming upwards made it as far as my knees before it receded with a roar that held more than a promise for the next one.

'I know . . . Not that it makes any difference,' I muttered wearily. We both knew there wasn't any decision left to take. If we jumped now the next sea could hurl us right back up like an express lift, pulverising us under the inverted super-structure in a red bloody foam. If we waited a few more minutes we could have a whole ship on top of us. Or most of a ship.

One thing we were guaranteed. We wouldn't have time to drown. Not like poor, lonely Nicholson out there.

'We stay!' I yelled as the next sea fell away in a rage of frustration. 'We stay right here, Bosun. Suddenly I feel . . .' I turned my head and forced a grin which must have looked like a Death's Head at a funeral. '. . . I feel *lucky*, god-dammit!'

He blinked at me for a moment. Then he stared hard at the seas which reared and screamed almost on a level with our eyes, and slowly arched his neck back until he could look up at the topsy turvy wreck which loomed three thousand tons high above us.

Then I saw the little captive pools of salt water trapped in the folds of his lifejacket start to dance and shimmer as his shoulders began to heave. The first rumbling guffaw, when it came, could only have been composed of pure undiluted irony.

I hoped the ship would hurry up and roll over on us while he was still enjoying himself. It would make a perfect end to a lousy year.

My legs began to shake uncontrollably as the fear clamped down on me. Closing my eyes I silently urged over and over again, 'I didn't really mean that bit about the ship hurrying up, God. Not *hurrying* up, anyway . . .'

Not that it made any difference. Just like Tanker always said.

In actual fact they'd all been lousy years. Ever since John had given up his appointment as a Royal Naval salvage officer and I'd relinquished command of one of Her Majesty's ocean salvage vessels to form, together, the Templeton Ross Towing Company — me being the end bit, the Ross part of the great adventure, partly because John had the brains but mainly because he had more money to put down as a deposit on a mortgaged-to-the-hilt, clapped-out old tugboat.

She still was, too. Mortgaged and clapped-out, I mean. All we'd managed to scrape together over the past six years were the interest payments. I estimated that, at the last accounting the only bits of *Tactician* which we actually owned were the starboard wheelhouse doors and three quarters of the bloody funnel.

And the barnacles on her hull. The ones which should have been scraped off along with the rust at her last scheduled drydocking. The one she never actually got because we needed the money for fuel oil and decipherable charts and generator spares instead.

And food. We appreciated how much it boosted the crew's morale, letting them eat every Monday and Thursday. It gave a completely new perspective to the expression 'skeleton crew' when you thought about it, and that's what *Tactician* was operating with — a minimal complement of case-hardened salvage men who'd stuck grimly with us for God only knew what motives. John put them down to loyalty and maybe with some of them, like Tanker and Barney Slough our Second Officer, it was, but personally I attributed them to something a little more practical — like the fact that we hadn't been able to pay them for the past two months and they wanted to be around to look after their involuntary investment.

In a nutshell, the Templeton Ross Towing empire was broke. All we needed to finish us was a writ nailed to the mast so that John and I could go back to driving other people's tugboats, and salvaging other people's casualties.

And to being a little sad because we'd lost a pride which we'd fought for six years to keep.

There *was* an alternative. Only one. And that was to catch up with every other salvage man's dream – to get a line aboard our very own Big One. Maybe that was partly why our crowd stayed too, for the day when the radio screamed MAYDAY from very close by, and we arrived first on the scene of disaster where a ship's crew are either too scared or too exhausted to save their own vessel and are forced to abandon her to the elements – or to us, the salvors.

One successful operation, and the salvage award arising from it would save us. We could survive to tilt at the Dragon again. Just one ship in trouble of our very own.

Which was why, when the eviscerated *Emperor Vespasian* cried to the world that she had been in collision and was abandoning, *Tactician* had bucketed crazily through a force ten gale to reach her first. And why, even when we got there to find that a lead-filled bucket had more reserve buoyancy left than our casualty, Tanker and Nicholson and I had still boarded her because she was the only thing between *Tactician* and a creditor's forced sale.

I hadn't let John come this time. He'd taken too many chances already on burning ships and wave-battered hulks and I knew that next time the Dragon would get him for sure.

And that was why I was waiting for the *Emperor Vespasian* to roll over on top of *me* instead.

I wasn't even telling the truth about feeling lucky. From where I stood all the odds seemed to be in favour of the Dragon.

Something dug hard into my ribs. I knew it wasn't big enough to be the ship or soft enough to be my imagination so I opened my eyes as Tanker jerked urgently with his elbow again and pointed aft along the sprawling, foam-lashed decks of our very temporary residence.

'Right astern! You see anything, Skipper?'

I bent over gingerly to peer over – or was it round? – the after bridge rail but all I could make out was a nightmare of tumbled, threshing derricks flailing like giant metronomes in time with the lurch of the wreck, and vacantly gaping ventilators staring out over distorted rails while, running in a wavy black fuel oil scar just below the fore and aft centre-line of the deck, the tide mark which showed just how far the sea had advanced already.

'Yeah!' I snapped, resenting his shaking me out of my lethargy and back into the nightmare. 'I can see now why I should've been a bloody farmer after I left school.'

Then I said, 'Sorry, Bosun,' because he didn't have any real reason at all for being here in the first place, and because Tanker knew better than any of us how this hopeless salvage attempt was doomed to failure before it ever started. But maybe Tanker had his own particular Dragon too, and he couldn't let anyone else tilt at it for him.

He never let his eyes stray from that point down aft for a moment. 'There's something out there, Skipper. Rounding our stern. It's got to be the tug, there ain't nothing else crazy enough to come in that close.'

Just for a moment I felt a surge of hope, but it didn't last. John would have had to be out of his mind to come near this wallowing death trap. As Tanker said, there were too many invisible hazards like trailing wire ropes to lock a turning propeller, and almost submerged derricks which would penetrate *Tactician*'s plating without . . .

Then Tanker bellowed, 'It is her. Goddammit it *is* her!' and I had my first sea-level view of my ship as she literally battered round the casualty's quarter in a buffeting turn which sent great sheets of white water cascading from under her high bow. And then a beam sea caught her, throwing her over to an impossible fifty degree angle which gave me time for a strangled 'Oh *Jesus*!' before she'd righted herself and

13

settled on a corkscrew course directly towards us.

I forgot about the ship hanging over us and watched in horrified fascination. One moment *Tactician*'s scarred red waterline reared high above our height of eye as she surfed over the crest of a mountain, then she was plunging down like an express train virtually to disappear with only the rounded plan of her stern showing black against the maelstrom. And up again with the boiling water piling up around the dirty brown island of her bridge . . . and submerging again . . .

. . . before a personal wave all of my own reared from the abyss below our perch, curling around my waist with icy fingers. And snatched me clean off the *Emperor Vespasian*'s bridge before I'd even time to start screaming with the shock of it!

I once sailed with an old Orcadian salvage hand whose very philosophy of life was that you only retained it for as long as the sea wished you to. And that if it ever claimed you, as that sea which reared over the *Vespasian* had taken me, then a man had only the divine right to do one merciful thing.

'Take a long, deep breath as ye go under, man,' he said quietly, with the lilt in his voice as soft as the caress of a blowing thistledown. 'Wi' your lungs full o' water the sea will be gentle and welcoming. There's a great peace to be found . . . once ye accept the inevitability of death.'

Two days later he was in an inflatable which capsized while taking a line to a North Sea oil rig. A helicopter from the rig plucked three men from the water before they'd had time to drift twenty yards from the spot. They were working on deck less than ten minutes after the accident.

They picked up an empty lifejacket, too. My old Orcadian must have deliberately slipped out of it even as the raft was going over. I often wondered if he ever found that peace which he said was at the bottom of the sea.

I wasn't quite that curious, though. Or fatalistic.

So I saved the scream for later and filled my lungs with air instead, just before the undertow dragged me down. I remember thinking it was certainly very quiet down there after the symphony from the breaking-up ship. Then I seemed to be falling at an incredible speed as the wave fell away until my head finally broke water and I had a brief image of Tanker's horrified features gazing down into the trough, the dome of his head projecting out over the underside of the wing, with the still-shiny brass of the starboard navigation light showing against the green painted side screen . . .

. . . while the lift started its trip up to the penthouse floor again and I went under thinking, 'You should be doing about forty knots by the time you hit that bloody nav. light, you poor inadequate bast . . . !'

Something smashed into my shoulder with crushing force and I think I did shriek then with the pain of it. Before I was strangled in mid-yell as a tourniquet clamped around my wind pipe while, at the same time, I was vaguely conscious of the sea's suction clawing in terrible frustration down the length of my body.

And then the sea fell away altogether and I wasn't a drowning man any more. I was a hanging man instead. Suspended over a raging cauldron with a ship for a gallows and my collar for a noose. I even had the knuckle of a hangman's knot grinding agonisingly under my ear.

By the time the next sea swamped in under me I'd gratefully started to black out, but it wasn't quite such a big one and it just gave my dangling body enough buoyancy to ease the strain around my neck.

From a long way away Tanker's voice was roaring incredibly, 'Make fast, Skipper . . . f'r God's sake, hang *on*, man . . . !' while a leg clamped across my chest like a steel vice and the knot eased from under my ear as the Bosun tentatively freed my screwed-up jersey.

I lay like a fish out of water, pinioned on my back with

one hand scrabbling for a grip and my legs still swinging over nothing. Gradually, disbelievingly, I forced one eye open and fought with the swimming optical spots twirling slowly round and round across my vision. The tipped-over wheelhouse of the *Emperor Vespasian* was back in its rightful place above me, but somehow it didn't seem so threatening this time.

One of the cavorting light blobs gave way to Tanker's wind-thrashed features gazing down at me with an uncertain mixture of disbelief, pride and sheer disgust at my ever having allowed myself to go over in the first place.

'I jus' grabbed at the water an' there you was,' he said, beginning to look a bit pleased with himself. 'Like a lucky dip. Just as the next wave lifted you back up.'

'You'd've been better off with a packet of barley sugar,' I spluttered faintly. Then I remembered and struggled to sit upright. '*Tactician!* Where the . . . !'

Another sea reared over me, burying me, but Tanker's leg was like a wire lashing. Having landed me he wasn't ever going to let me go again, though I vaguely hoped he wouldn't be too dogmatic when our island finally sank.

He gestured laconically with his chin. 'Only a couple've cables off, now, an' still coming at us like the clappers. Mad bastards the lot of 'em.'

They could be dead ones too, I thought dully, if John brought her in much closer. One fractional miscalculation, one following sea on her quarter at just the wrong moment and she'd be driven uncontrollably in under the overhang of the wreck's superstructure. Then the sea would lift her, but she wouldn't be able to rise with it because she'd be trapped by a sluggish, three thousand ton ceiling . . .

Tanker tugged at the straps on his lifejacket and a moment later it fluttered down past me to be lost in the welter of foam below. I caught his eye and he grinned without any humour at all. 'I won't need that any more,' he said calmly. 'Either way I don't need that.'

I thought about my old Orcadian, but it was too late to stop him now so I just nodded through the spray hanging between us and said, 'No, Tanker. Not any more.'

Then he helped me to my feet and we pressed back against the deck, feeling the warmth of each other's body, and waiting for the inevitable to happen. Once John committed himself to the manœuvre he had to complete it. And he had to be lucky as well. For our part we would only have one split second in which to jump – after that there would only be a grinding, obliterating gap between the two vessels, opening wider and wider again as she pulled away. If she ever did.

The Dragon parted its fangs in welcome, leering anticipatorily up at me.

Tanker tensed beside me, leaning forward slightly and ready. 'D'you want to go first?'

I didn't take my eyes off the tug, now less than a hundred yards off and still boring in under full power. 'Who needs to be a gentleman? Pick your own moment, Tanker boy, forget about me.'

Seventy yards. Sixty. I could see John's face a white blob behind the wheelhouse clearview screen. There were yellow oilskinned figures clinging grimly along her bucketing after deck, too. And I could make out the inverted towing hook aft, just as she slewed round a bit, but I hoped I wouldn't land on that . . .

Fifty yards.

'Forty!

The faint tinkle of her telegraphs carried over the narrowing gap between us and, immediately, a splurge of threshing foam kicked under her stern as she went astern. A sea parted under her and she fell away into a twenty foot trough until we were staring almost vertically down on to her streaming foredeck, but it was still too far to jump . . .

Ten yards and she was shuddering violently under astern power with her funnel exhaust roaring and spitting as she started to slew broadside to us with her wheel hard over . . .

then she was juggernauting upwards and inwards all at the same time with another crucifying sea building along her outboard side . . .

Tanker shouted, '*Christ!* He's not going to make it!'

A horrifying glimpse of her after deck sliding crazily in right *under* the flimsy structure we were marooned on, with the yellow oilskins scattering from the point of impact, and a fleeting impression of a chequerboard jumble of mattresses waiting for us . . .

I screamed frantically, '*GO . . . !*'

Then launched myself out into space.

Just as the half-ship turned completely upside down. And started to sink on top of us.

Ships die in a lot of different ways. Just like people. I know, I've seen a lot of them going, both ships and men.

Sometimes they go quietly, without being a trouble to anyone at all, slipping under the water with only an apologetic ripple to mark their passing. Others die more violently with a terrible rage inside them, still clawing at the surface of the sea with huge, boiling fingers long after they've gone. Those can be the dangerous ships. They can kill you. They are the ones which often catch you unawares and drag you down with them, locked inside a tormented, booming steel coffin.

They blow into spinning, super-heated fragments in War or sometimes just lie over in tired submission during Peace. Some ships, like gas-filled tankers, blow up at any time at all. You can't trust ships, not when they have the touch of death on them.

The *Emperor Vespasian* had a character all of her own. When she was wounded at first she bore it with dignity, refusing to submit immediately even when the wound became mortal as the sea swamped into her forward hold and overpowered her. She sacrificed Nicholson as a sop to the Dragon but she still protected Tanker and I.

Until we spurned her.

And then she tried to kill us with a dreadful anger.

I remember the horror of seemingly being suspended in mid-air as the tug hesitated at the top of the crest before starting to plummet from below me with appalling speed. Then I caught up with it, and even as I went forward into a water-floating mattress in a paratrooper's half-roll I realised that, had I been going down as the after deck was still skyrocketing, the impact would have shattered my legs irreparably.

Or killed me outright. If I'd still been a little bit lucky.

Strangely there was still a ceiling above me though, and I thought irritably, '*That*'s a bit bloody outrageous after all we've . . .' Then a naked black man cannoned into me, slamming me forward into a dazed and even more outraged bundle against the after end of the towing winch.

A voice in my head kept complaining 'But we don't *have* any black men aboard *Tactician*. With or without bloody clothes!' while all the time someone was trying to wedge me further and further in under the winch barrel while screaming in my ear, 'Get back, Mister Ross! Jus' stay there an' hang *on* f'r . . .'

I'd only just found out that my inexplicable assailant was neither black nor naked, but that it was the wetsuit-clad figure of our senior diver Mike Tracey, when the finally rolling *Emperor Vespasian*'s bridge wing thundered down towards the mattress on which I'd recently landed.

And then it was back to square one for Captain Ross, unsuccessful salvage king, as the rest of the capsizing ship followed in a rumbling, avalanching procession which battered my already bruised mind into a shocked acceptance that the old Orcadian had been right all the time, and that there wasn't any point in fighting the sea – not when it really wanted to claim you for its own.

I remember that familiar bridge wing buckling and splintering as it telescoped into our after deck with the strong-backs of the transverse towing bars slicing great gashes up the length of it. Then I thought about Tanker and started shouting, 'The Bosun! Where the hell's the *Bosun* . . .?' but nobody could have heard me above the nightmare which was tearing us apart, or if they did they were past the stage of caring about anything or anyone any more.

Beneath me the tug reared like an animal in pain burying her stern under the weight of the sinking casualty. Somewhere a man was sobbing in a high-pitched key which slashed across the cacophony of water thundering in over our counter. Then the water rolled over me, too, and I couldn't stand it any longer so I just ground my face into the oily filth under the winch and waited for the Dragon.

And waited.

But it didn't come. Only the sickness. And that was washed away by the sea too quickly to notice.

Instead I was aware of the water receding in excited, gurgling little tributaries from around the base of my refuge. Abruptly the deck slammed up into me as our stern started to surface like a cork until the gurgling went away and was replaced once more by the bedlam from the sinking ship astern of us.

Astern of us . . . ?

Tanker's voice roared petulantly above the din, 'Gerroff me! Get bloody *off've* me, dammit!'

I started to laugh. And cry. The cold rubbery skin of Tracey's wetsuit stirred against my face as he ever so doubt-fully began to rise. There was only one thing left to do.

So I did it.

I stuck two derisive fingers up towards the Dragon.

CHAPTER TWO

The weather hadn't improved one bit in the twenty-four hours since the spreading oil slick had faded astern.

It was casualty weather. Salvage man's weather. The kind of weather which saw the ocean tugs racing seawards in hungry optimism while other ships wallowed towards shelter. Yet even that promise didn't seem quite so important, in a way. Not now the first crushing disappointment had given way to the tentative acceptance that we really were still alive and more or less undamaged.

There was Nicholson, of course. But he himself had chosen the game. No regrets could help him any more. So there was a certain element of wry consolation in the warm atmosphere of the wheelhouse on that bleak Mediterranean December morning. We reckoned we still had at least one vital asset left – we just had to be the luckiest paupers in the salvage game.

We couldn't have known that, right then, even our luck was starting to run out too.

'Did you hear that?' John called, suddenly half-turning towards us. Until a rogue sea hoisted our starboard bow high above the line of the horizon and my co-director, his coffee mug and most of the other inanimate objects hit the forward windows with a crash.

I grinned furtively at Tanker as he rolled to the punch, automatically giving her a few spokes of starboard wheel and bringing her head up before she'd time to fall off. He sort of winked back then his eyes fell to the steering compass again while a spatter of spray rattled the glass. The spray didn't make as much noise as John's head.

'Hear what?' I queried, feeling a bit guilty about the grin because, next time, it could just as easily be my skull and my breakfast coffee.

John lurched across the wheelhouse, reaching for the volume control on the VHF transceiver. A surge of static filled the air, the sort of noise you hear when you put your ear to a seashell, only much louder.

'Sounded like a Mayday call,' he muttered irritably, probing his forehead with a doubtful finger. 'Distress transmission. Channel Sixteen.'

Tactician buried her head into another vicious sea, almost grinding to a halt with the impact, but John was ready for it this time and just caressed the mute control until the static died to a soft splutter. That was all there was, though. Just the static.

He shrugged at me. 'Thought it was a Mayday. For a minute.' He looked disappointed. So did Tanker behind the wheel.

I grinned again and punched him gently on the shoulder. A grey roller rose hugely above the port bridge window, glared balefully at me through a foam-streaked eye, then subsided again in sullen defeat. 'We're going home, John, remember? Gib, Falmouth then – if we can con Charlie Stutz into a buckshee load of fuel – it's up into the wide grey North Sea to find whose rigs need towing. The hell with "No cure, no pay" salvage contacts 'til we build up some capital.'

But it was disappointing, all the same. That nobody was sinking or on fire, or dropping a propeller within VHF range – not that we wished anyone bad fortune, of course, or not more than any bankrupt doctor sitting in an unattended surgery, or an undertaker with rather more coffins than cadavers.

It was just that we both knew that Charlie Stutz wouldn't give us credit on a pint of milk, never mind a full bunker. And that, even if he did, we'd still never get past Falmouth dockhead before the bailiffs padlocked us to the first mooring

ring, which meant that *Tactician* was virtually making her very last passage under the tattered house flag of the Templeton Ross Towing Company.

But I was still adamant about one thing, John was too. We both agreed implicitly that we were never, ever going to risk our necks again in attempting to save some screwed-up hulk just because the salvage award could keep us in what was a bloody rotten business anyway.

At long last we'd finally learnt sense. At last we'd developed into mature, responsible people.

Then the VHF screamed quite positively . . . AYDAY . . . MAYDAY . . . MAYDAY . . . ! And the mature, responsible people fell over each other trying to make it first to the transmitter!

So someone *was* in trouble after all. A comber broke green over *Tactician*'s foredeck and thundered against the bridge front. The radio pleaded urgently for a second time . . . ALL SHIPS . . . MAYDAY . . . *MAYDAY* . . . and I caught the glint of sympathy in John's eyes as he started to answer.

Someone was in big trouble. Storm force trouble.

And if they were within VHF range, then they weren't very far away.

I think we'd both known in our hearts that we were only making a gesture. That neither John nor I were capable of ignoring the basic reactions of every salvage man in the world to a distress plea – to dive for the chart, plot speed, time and distance to the still anonymous casualty. Then go like hell.

It wasn't only for gain, it was for something stronger than that. The overpowering bitterness I'd felt as I watched the *Emperor Vespasian* going down wasn't only because she dragged what seemed to be the last of our dream down with her. There was a sadness too, that was more for her dying than for our future.

So we hadn't really meant what we said after we'd stood

silently on the after deck of *Tactician* and watched the great carcase rolling faster and faster into the gouting, foam-lashed sea so close astern that I could reach out and touch her for one last gesture before she went.

John had raced down the bridge ladder three at a time the moment we'd cleared the wreck, his face reflecting an emotion I'd never seen before. Then he'd heard Tanker's unrepentant bellow and caught sight of Tracey hauling me groggily from under the winch, so he started to grin like a bloody idiot, picking his way across the wreckage-littered afterdeck and round the splintered, torn-away section of *Vespasian*'s bridge wing which had surrendered just before it had managed to drag us down.

But we stopped as he saw me staring aft, and maybe there was something he'd never seen in my face either. Putting his hand on my shoulder he'd just said quietly, 'It doesn't matter, Peter. Right now it doesn't matter a damn.'

I hadn't answered immediately. I'd watched the arcing funnel falling towards us until it smashed flat against the sea in an exploding gout of spray and billowing carbon soot while an abandoned lifeboat careered end over end down the vertical boat deck, trying outrageously to catch up with the rest of the ship. Then the after mast thrashing under with the derricks reared towards the sky and one steel spar pointing accusingly at us for letting her die like that . . .

Abruptly the tidal wave she'd displaced caught up with us, flinging our counter high in the air and, for one terrifying second, causing us to wonder if we really had escaped from the Dragon after all.

Then it had passed below us and I could see the abandoned ship again, now simply a flat, rust-obscene, upside-down whale breaking the surface with the waves merely undulating mountains reflecting the black gloss of oil which smothered them.

I turned away. John was watching me inquiringly and I knew we couldn't risk fighting the Dragon any longer. Not

24

without proper equipment and the sort of capital which would allow us to stay clear of the really dangerous ones. The killer ships.

'That's the last one,' I muttered tightly. 'The very last one, Johnny . . . Agreed?'

It seemed so easy to say. At the time.

VHF reception was bad. But so was our set.

John said clearly, 'This is salvage tug *Tactician*. We hear you strength three . . . go ahead . . . Over!'

He released the pressel switch and the static came back, lost occasionally against the background howl of the wind and sea. I couldn't smother a cynical grin as I noticed, after all our good resolutions, the way he chewed nervously at his lower lip and the way Tanker half turned from the wheel, watching the set fiercely as if commanding it to answer again.

Bending over the chart I picked up the dividers, measuring our distance run from the last estimated position. It placed us ten miles off the North African coast and east of Cape Bougaroni. I marked the current EP and noted the time beside it – 0628. *Tactician* shuddered and my pencil made an involuntary little dribble towards Algiers.

I muttered 'Dammit!' and reached for the rubber. Then forgot about the chart because the static went away and a shipwrecked stranger started talking to us again.

. . . OTOR VESSEL SARIKAMIS . . . ARE AGROUND ON RO . . . EST RAS OUM AHI . . . until the set began to crackle and spit hysterically as the text of the message was lost under a welter of interference.

John snarled bitterly, 'Oh, *shit*!' and slammed the VHF with the palm of his hand. It yelled . . . ISTANCE URGENTLY REQUIRED . . . back at him then sullenly refused to have any more to do with us. I didn't blame it, it should have been retired from active service long ago anyway.

I frowned at the chart. 'Where the hell's Est Ras Oum whatsit? *If* that's where she's ashore in the first place.'

Tanker held her head into a breaking crest. 'Oum Ahee or Assey it was, Skipper.'

'We need a new VHF,' John growled petulantly.

'We *need* a new ship,' I snapped back, 'but *that*'s irrelevant too in view of the prospects . . . Unless we can find that casualty out there an' get a line aboard.'

John looked innocent. 'Thought we'd agreed. No more Lloyd's Open Forms. No cure, no pay?'

I said heavily, 'Ha bloody ha!' It wasn't exactly a gem of repartee but with him being a hypocrite too there didn't seem much point.

The sea chuckled at our frustration, then positively roared with spiteful glee as it piled in a welter of broken water over the bows. John called 'Sarikamis – this is Tactician . . . Come in Sarikamis . . . !' while I stared gloomily through the clear view screen and debated on whether to slow her down to save fuel or not. And thought about those faceless sailors out there who might drown in the next few hours because Templeton Ross Towing couldn't even afford a decent radio set . . .

Radio!

I reached for the radio cabin phone at the same time as John. Just for a moment we grinned at each other sheepishly – one of the primary tools of the salvage trade is a high-powered communications room listening in around the clock, and even we had managed to keep our main radio equipment on top line. The recently expired VHF bridge set was largely for harbour and close range ship-to-ship working.

Not normally for distress calls. But that never really occurred to us. Not right then, anyway.

Eddie Styles, our Chief Operator, answered. I couldn't keep the peevishness out of my voice. 'That Mayday call. Why didn't you report it, Sparks?'

There was a moment's hesitation, then his voice with a touch of asperity. 'There was a dago tanker yellin' from off Pesaro but that's up in the Adriatic i'nt it? We'd need jet engines to get that far in time, Skipper.'

I said sharply, 'When was that call?'

'I logged it in at . . . zero five four two. Over half an hour ago. But how did you . . .'

I frowned. 'There's been nothing since then?'

'Nothing! But how did you know about the tanker, Skip? Her call was on WT, pretty weak at that. Your bridge set couldn't . . .'

'We got a call two minutes ago on the VHF,' I said carefully. 'That means she can't be much more than twenty, twenty-five miles away. It should've blown your ears off on your set.'

Eddie almost shrugged at me down the phone. 'Unless they've lost their radio room and only have a bridge set left, Skipper. I'll keep listening watch, that's all I can do.'

'If she does call again try and get a fix on her, Eddie. And let me know right away.'

I hung up and turned away thoughtfully. John was bent over the chart. I watched as he drew a circle around our present position with a radius of twenty-five miles. He tapped the pencilled ring. 'If the *Sarikamis* was calling, then she's within that area somewhere.'

'She's there,' I muttered positively. 'Probably ashore between, say, Bougaroni and . . . Djidjelli. And God help them.'

He looked up at me, the chart table Anglepoise carving his features into grim, highlighted planes. He knew what I meant. That little bit of the Algerian Coast had everything a Cornish wrecker could possibly ask for. Great sheer cliffs which dropped vertically to the sea, outcrops of submerged rocks which reached out for you like invisible fingers . . .

I stabbed at the chart. 'Ras oum Achiche! That's what the man said, wasn't it?'

'Est Ras oum something, yeah!'

'*West* Ras oum Achiche.' I grinned fiercely. 'So many miles *west* of there. We've got her, Johnny Boy. And within

27

less than two hours' steaming. It can't be more or she'd have been out of VHF range.'

John chewed his lip again. 'Our radar's U/S. It's a bad coast to feel our way into without it.'

I shrugged. It was getting to be the fashionable gesture aboard *Tactician*. It was a substitute for calculating the odds against us, then ignoring them. 'And do *you* think we should keep off, John?'

He smiled. It was a soft, wry sort of smile.

'No!' he murmured, quite positively.

I didn't say anything for a moment, then I caught sight of Tanker's head lifted like a pointer sniffing the scent. I called, 'O.K.! Down, Fido! Steady as she goes 'til we clear Bougaroni, then I'll give you a course for somewhere or other.'

We were all grinning now, like schoolkids going to an unexpected treat. The Dragon had thrown down the gauntlet yet again, and we hadn't been able to resist picking it up.

Funnily enough, I think it was at that particular moment that I also felt the first vague sense of unease. The feeling that there was something not quite right about the situation.

Something to do with an unknown ship called the *Sarikamis.*

The cliffs of Bougaroni had reared up on our port beam exactly on schedule, their base lost in the white foam whipped up by the gale and their tops equally nebulous as the black rock face faded into the grey spindrift of the early morning.

Most of the crowd were on deck by now, hunched against the spray in their yellow oilskins but with every eye searching anxiously along the hazy shoreline for the first sign of any break which could mean a beached wreck. Pressed against the wheelhouse window I could make out Mike Tracey, clinging disdainfully to our stemhead with the water cascading in runnels down his inevitable wetsuit and a sort of 'Eff you, Jack – I'm waterproof' expression on his face.

I wondered if he wore it to dinner dances and funerals, too.

The casualty – if there really was a casualty – hadn't spoken to us again since. John had wanted to call her on the big set but we'd decided against it because, if we tried, then every other salvage tug in the Southern Mediterranean would have homed in on us. And it was pretty safe to expect that, if her own equipment had been working, she'd have been yelling her head off in fright anyway.

Or so we assumed.

The only thing we were certain of was that a ship called the *Sarikamis* did exist. John had checked her out in our last year's copy of Lloyd's. It didn't tell us much but it gave us hope of rich pickings if we found her – and if she was salvable even then.

'She's Turkish! Eight thousand three hundred tons gross . . . conventional dry cargo . . . built 1964 . . . sounds good if it's her – that recent she could stand a fair pounding.'

'She'll need to,' I said gloomily, glancing at the huge westerly swell reaching into the shore, 'Who're her owners?'

He disappeared into the book again. 'Officially Hazar, Melen and Company. But nearly forty per cent of the Turkish merchant fleet are part-financed by their Maritime Bank . . . uh . . . *Denizcilik Bankasi*, isn't it?'

I pretended not to hear him. Personally I couldn't even *say* it, never mind remember it. I tapped the chart with the dividers. 'My guess is that she's there somewhere . . . though God knows how they managed to do it, unless they're blind.'

The point of the dividers rested on a vicious little cluster of rocks marked about half a mile to seaward of the tideline. The symbols showed sand inshore up to the base of vertical cliffs. It was pure guesswork on my part – she could be anywhere within ten miles of that spot – but we had to have some starting point for the search, and her Mayday had inferred she was 'Aground on rocks!' A just-awash outcrop like that, with deep water to seaward, could quite conceivably fit the description.

John looked unconvinced, or maybe he was just being awkward because I wasn't impressed with his Turkish general knowledge. 'It's a lee shore certainly. Not many lights to get a fix. But she must have drifted a helluva lot further inside her course line than they estimated . . .'

I frowned uncomfortably. That was the one big flaw which didn't make sense. For any ship to have drifted that far in it meant that she had to be a good twelve *miles* south of her watchkeeper's reckoning . . . the uneasy feeling came back even stronger than before.

John looked at me pointedly. 'Though they *could* have been blind, couldn't they?'

I couldn't shake that damned uneasiness off. 'Eh?'

He grinned boyishly. 'If their radar was on the blink, too . . . just like ours?'

I rode the jibe with lofty dignity. 'It so happens that it would have been pitch dark when they hit. And *we* also happen to know precisely where we are.'

He nodded ambiguously and glanced past me, down at the chart. A curling following sea swung our stern and I heard Tanker mutter darkly as he spun the wheel. Then John spoke again, but this time there wasn't any jocularity in his tone. There was something else indefinable – something which betrayed that he too had a growing awareness that things were, somehow, going wrong.

'It doesn't add up, dammit! She yells for help – but only on VHF. She says she's aground – yet the only way she could be this far inshore is by drifting twelve miles . . . twelve *miles*, Peter . . . off course.'

I spread my hands. 'It could happen. We've seen ships go down twenty miles from where they thought they were at the time.'

He shook his head. 'They were almost always accumulated errors. A few degrees' drift over a long distance which adds up to a major mistake . . . this is different and you know it. Look at the chart, Peter. Any ship intending to pass off Cape

Bougaroni and going wrong would have hit close to the point – not several miles into the bay.'

I started to get stubborn – or maybe I didn't want to believe we were really only chasing a forlorn hope. 'She could have been heading for Djidjelli, maybe even Bejaia. That would have meant a good twenty degree alteration abeam of the Cape.'

'Yet that, in *its* turn, means that they knew exactly where they were before they made it . . . so we're back to square bloody one!'

I turned away from the chart and stared ahead to where the curve of the shoreline was still lost against the neutral grey-ness of the morning. I saw the crew out there, too. Still watching and waiting, and hoping. We had less than an hour's run to my point marked 'X'. And to a potential treasure trove called the *Sarikamis*, if my wild hunch was right.

'I want to go on, at least 'til we're past Ras oum Achiche, John. Then we'll be sure, one way or the other.'

He didn't argue any more. There wasn't a lot he could say.

Because whatever the illogicality of it, we had undoubtedly picked up a plea from a vessel in distress – not only John and I but also Tanker had heard it. So somebody must have sent it out.

And they *must* have sent it from not too far away.

But there wasn't anybody there at all. Not even after we'd run eight miles past Ras oum Achiche with every pair of eyes on board scanning through the ever worsening visibility for any sign, any faint indication that there had ever been a recent wreck between Bougaroni and the port of Djidjelli to the west.

No oil slick. No flotsam. No lifebelts or splintered hatch covers. No waterlogged corpses floating limply in the swell.

No *Sarikamis*! It was as straightforward as that . . . or we had misinterpreted the static-tortured contents of that crazy Mayday call, and she was somewhere – anywhere – up to fifty miles astern instead, pounding herself and her crew to fragments without any hope of rescue because Captain Peter Ross, salvage man shortly to be retired, had miscalculated yet again.

So we turned around and steamed back towards Bougaroni. I was beginning to hate even the name of the bloody place. But we didn't have any choice now, John knew that too, because it wasn't just a question of salvage. There were men's lives at stake, or there had been three hours before – when that Mayday was sent . . .

. . . and it *was* sent!

As we came up towards my spot marked 'X' for the second time the visibility had clamped down to less than a mile, with great phalanxes of solid rain marching across the bay to seaward and even the black cliffs curving round across our bows almost invisible through the murk.

John wore a faint but sympathetically concealed 'I told you so' air. Tanker, now stubbornly back on the wheel, wore a glowering expression which suggested the Turks were all the bloody same anyway, all mouth an' no action. The crowd out on deck wore anything they could dream up to keep the driving rain out, from sou'westers and oilskins to cavernous macintoshes with odd things like *Plymouth Public Lighting Department* and *Glasgow Corporation* embroidered accusingly across the collar lapels. And frogmen's gear, of course – really the only acceptable attire to be seen in on a wet day off the coast of North Africa.

I wore what I fondly hoped was a casual 'In complete command of the situation' look – to cover up the gnawing anxiety I really felt at being this close to a lee shore in this kind of weather. That, and my still ever-present sense of unease over our reasons for being here in the first place.

I kept well clear of that cluster of rocks shown on the chart. We didn't need a picture to tell us where they were, for that matter. One glance shorewards revealed a boiling, leprous sore running along the surface of the sea for maybe quarter of a mile while occasionally, as a crest collapsed into itself in a racing, thundering spume, black fangs from the reef seemed to rise up and snarl towards us before submerging again to await a more unwary prey.

They already had a name according to the chart – some Arabic legend – but I gave them an identity of my own right then. It was a name I'll never be able to forget, not after the events which were, even then, beginning to overwhelm us.

The Scab Rocks!

Something made me write it alongside the symbols on that chart. *The Scab . . . !* And all of a sudden I felt very, very cold.

And I didn't know why, but the hair on the nape of my neck started to prickle with an unreasoning dread of that storm-swept place which had called to us so strangely.

I said shakily, 'Nothing! Not a bloody sign of anything . . . !'

Then John shouted tightly, 'Look! For'rad of the beam . . . it's a ship. Coming in from seaward . . .'

He broke off, his face a mask of slowly dawning incredulity. Then, while Tanker and I were still swinging towards the port windows and trying desperately to pierce that hanging monochrome opacity enveloping us, he added in a barely controlled whisper, 'But she's still at full speed . . .

. . . and she's steering straight for the goddamned *cliffs*!'

CHAPTER THREE

We were watching a ghost ship. A supernatural, shimmering phantom floating above the surface of the sea itself. A ship with no substance and only the outline of masts and upper-works and funnel to show there was anything materialising out there at all.

No one moved. No one spoke. Inside the wheelhouse my pencil dribbled back and forward, back and forward in time with the roll of the tug but I didn't make any move to stop it, I just stared through the streaming windows at that distant apparition and felt utterly bewildered and a little frightened, too.

For a moment.

Until Tanker's muttered 'Jes*us*!' broke the spell.

While the shape assumed a third dimension as the stranger burst through the blowing mists of rain until we could make out the details of lifeboats and ventilators and ochre-painted derricks still secured for sea. We could make out, too, the white bone in her teeth which reared up and over the long fo'c'slehead to sheet aft over her superstructure in flying clouds of spray – the bow wave which, at first sight, had merged with the broken water to give her the appearance of being suspended in space.

A bow wave which could only be created by engines driving at full speed. And on a die-straight course towards the vertical rock face which we could only barely distinguish ourselves and which, from her position further off, she would still be unable to see.

Not unless she was running on radar, and then the solution to the mystery was simple . . . her watchkeepers were all either dead, mad or unbelievably incompetent.

Either way, she would run out of deep water in less than two miles. Steaming as she was at, say, eighteen knots it meant she had less than six minutes to live.

Maybe five or six more for most of her crew, in that berserk sea clawing at the base of Ras oum Achiche – excluding those really fortunate ones killed outright by the impact!

I yelled, 'Flares, John! Reds, greens – anything to attract her attention . . .' then I hit Channel Sixteen on the VHF but this time there wasn't even the usual splutter of static. It was as dead as . . . I caught sight of the other ship, a lot closer already, and thought of a couple of pretty appropriate similes before throwing the radio handphone down and diving for the Aldis box instead.

Tanker was watching me questioningly over his shoulder. I started struggling to disentangle the Aldis cord which was twisted into its usual bloody Chinese puzzle like it always was when you needed it in a hurry.

'Ring on for full speed, Bosun.' I glanced out of the starboard window – the rocks, my Scab Rocks, were just pulling abeam now about half a mile inshore of us, 'But keep her steady as she goes. Understand?'

He said, 'Aye, aye! Steady as she goes, Skipper!' as calmly as if I'd just told him to nip below for a smoke. I was grateful for the show of faith – I'd just told him to keep us on a course which would place us precisely between the unknown freighter and the cliffs.

By closing the angle of deflection it would increase their chances of seeing our warnings as we came dead ahead of them. I tried not to think what might happen if they still kept on going – it would make *Tactician* into the biggest fender in the Mediterranean.

Or under it.

One thing f'r sure. Our bank manager would be a bit bloody angry . . .

Barney Slough, the Second Mate, came bursting into the wheelhouse yelling *'Ashipontheporthea . . .'*

I threw the Aldis at him and snarled back, 'So unravel this bloody thing an' start flashing "U" . . . You are standing into danger!' Then I grabbed for the radio-room phone instead, feeling the nervous sweat running down the side of my nose and the deck throbbing more and more urgently under my feet as the revs built up to full power.

'Come on, Sparks! Come *on* f'r . . . !'

The first flare went up with a *whoooosh* but I wasn't really aware of it. I was too busy watching that crazily closing ship out there, now less than a mile off and still steaming headlong into Africa without the slightest indication that there was anyone aboard who gave a damn.

I had a brief vision of how horribly normal things must seem to the majority of her crew who, like all ship's crews, wouldn't even give a second thought to the situation outside their immediate day-to-day environment. The watch-below men, now either finishing a leisurely late breakfast in the Formica-shiny mess room or relaxing with heads down in their bunks. Her engineers below decks, secure amid the pounding roar of engines which had probably never faltered in their familiar beat since the last port of call. The daywork hands, skiving under cover in bosun's stores and paint lockers and not bothering to glance outside because they'd already seen the sea yesterday and the day before that, and the monotonous day before that . . .

I started to feel sick with apprehension and jiggled the wireless-room receiver savagely. What the hell *was* Eddie doing back there? Feet up on the transmitter desk probably, paperback in hand and utterly unaware of the drama unfolding on the other side of his centrally-heated cocoon.

Which took me back to those complacent voyagers with the switched-off reflexes — until ten thousand tons of barrelling steel came to a dead stop against an immovable object with enough impact to project a standing man maybe fifty, sixty feet. And the main engines sheared from their bedplates and kept on going through to the bows while the after end started to telescope just in time to meet half a cliff falling outwards and downwards and on to . . . !

Eddie's remote voice said resignedly, 'Radio room! An' I still haven't heard anoth . . . !'

Three quarters of a mile to go!

Another flare ripped skywards from our wing, bursting with a fuzzy *plop* out of sight.

I ground savagely, 'Shut up an' listen, Styles! Start transmitting immediately on open R/T . . . UNKNOWN SHIP IN AREA RAS OUM ACHICHE . . . DIVERT IMMEDIATELY . . . DIVERT . . . DIVERT . . .'

Eddie said, 'Eh?'

Oh *Christ*!

John's tight shout from the wing. 'She's altering! By God but she's finally turning, Peter.'

I dropped the handset and hurled myself past Barney and the nervously clacking Aldis, out to the wing where John stood in the driving rain with the black hair plastered across his face and a still-smoking empty flare cartridge in his outstretched hand.

From the wheelhouse, Tanker's coldly detached forecast. 'She still ain't goin' to make it though. Not now.'

On our spray-swept after deck a cluster of men clearing away the Avon S/550 inflatable and shipping the 65-horse Mercury outboard on its transom. Tracey's wetsuit gleaming like black varnish between a *Scottish Gas Board* raincoat and the Second Engineer's deerstalker as the three of them struggled with the big scrambling net. No need to ask if they thought that outrageous vessel had a hope in hell of scraping past Algeria, anyway.

Though she *was* swinging hard now, veering crazily towards us under full starboard helm, with the spray buffeting in great curving sheets from under her weather bow and the angle of her decks increasing steadily until we could almost see into her listing funnel-top.

I started to feel nervous for an entirely different reason

now. The way she was sheering towards us meant we would soon be in her path — if she didn't rip the full length of her exposed belly on the base of those looming cliffs first. But there wasn't much I could do right then, apart from maintain speed to give me manœuvrability. And pray!

She was half a mile ahead of us now, forming one point of an equilateral triangle with the sheer rock faces as the apex and our own position completing the geometry. And the triangle was getting smaller all the time as the three of us came closer and closer to convergence.

It was time to get out of it.

I shouted, 'I want sea room, Tanker. Port twenty the wheel!'

Someone said in a hushed voice, 'They've had it, all right. She's going in.'

Absently I noticed the crew on deck. Suddenly they weren't moving any more, just lining the bulwarks and watching silently, some chewing in savage unawareness at horny thumbnails while others were merely indicating the tension within them by the white clenched knuckles gripping the scarred rails.

She was fighting now, though. By God but that great ship was fighting to keep clear. Swinging round towards us with a smashed, flattened lee of water to mark her broadside. Clawing for offing under full astern power on her starboard engine while the other screw still raced ahead, driving her even tighter round until she was almost running parallel with — but still far too close to — the place which would kill her if it even stroked at her vitals.

One hundred yards off!

Seventy-five . . . ! Only white hysterical water now between the high slab sides and . . .

Someone thrust a pair of binoculars into my hands, I don't know who, so I swung them to my eyes even though I wasn't really sure of wanting to make out the closer, more intimate detail of a death blow.

Shocking in its impact, the optical distance between me and that careering freighter instantaneously divided by ten.

Tactician reared temperamentally, startled as the sea came under her turning bows. I had one madly gyrating image of dark-skinned, disbelieving faces staring downwards from the newcomer's boat deck at the still ever decreasing margin between them and a frightful death . . . then a blur of rusted black steel plating ending in a sudden gout of spouting water, forcing me to recoil involuntarily until I realised I was staring in close-up at her port engine discharge just above the water-line.

Beside me John whispered, 'She's going to tear her double bottoms out. Honest to . . . ! There's just no bloody sea room *left* for her!'

But I wasn't really listening any more.

My binoculars had just come to rest on the white-painted letters under her flared bows. They were very easy to read, magnified ten times like that.

They told me that rampaging ship's identity.

According to them her name was the . . . *SARIKAMIS.*

When one man fought with another, in the middle of a crisis.

With the astern power of two engines the *Sarikamis* was slowing down quite considerably by the time she had started to settle on a heading to pass across our bows from right to left. I suppose she could only have been making five knots as she arrived at a position about a quarter of a mile to seaward of us, over to starboard, and with a turbulent, creaming flower of agitated wash spreading outwards from her wake.

I'd just said, 'Telegraphs, Barney. Bring us down to slow ahead until she crosses,' when my binoculars settled on the Turk's bridge.

Her radar scanner was the first thing I noticed, still rotating smooth as silk above the forward end of the wheelhouse. I frowned thoughtfully – the mere fact that it *was* operating suggested that, as far as her watchkeepers were aware anyway, the *Sarikamis*'s radar was perfectly serviceable.

Yet the facts said it couldn't have been – or, alternatively, that it must have revealed those cliffs across her path from over thirty miles away.

But then I saw a man, a little man leaning out over the wing of her bridge and seemingly staring aft down the length of her. And almost immediately another man moved up behind him, from out of the wheelhouse itself, until the two figures merged in perspective . . .

. . . when suddenly, after what might or might not have been a brief struggle out there, seventy feet above the surface of the sea, there was only one toy figure left. And he seemed to run back towards the wheelhouse doors at the precise moment when the maelstrom under her stern ceased . . . died to a sullen swirl as she coasted away from it . . .

. . . then kicked up again a renewed frenzy as her engines were rung from full astern to full ahead once more.

I said in growing perplexity, 'That was a bit odd.'

John was frowning too. 'Moving ahead again? Yeah! I'd've thought they would have found out just where the bloody hell they really were before they charged around any more.'

I shook my head. 'No. That business up on her bridge . . . Those two characters?'

He shrugged, not really knowing what I meant. 'Too far away without glasses . . . But *what* the . . . ? Peter, look!'

I stopped wondering ..bout the vanishing man on the Turk's bridge and glanced at him in surprise. The tight snap in his voice was even more marked when he spoke again.

'She's turning, dammit. But she's altering towards us, Peter . . . That bloody madman's heading *inshore* again!'

And she was, too. And starting to build up speed as she swung to meet us, the long low profile of her shortening more and more through the veil of rain with every revolution of those huge propellers.

I went through our wheelhouse door like an express train, grabbing for the telegraph. We needed power too, now. All the thrust we could get to give me maximum manœuvrability to dodge that prowling freighter out there. Because somehow I knew, in that first disbelieving moment while the *Sarikamis* was still struggling to increase momentum after having slowed down, that we were to be her next target.

That there *was* insanity present in that storm-lashed bay off the North African coast after all. But that it didn't exist aboard *Tactician*. It had seized hold aboard a careering juggernaut five hundred yards away instead.

And that in the next three or four minutes I was going to have to play a freakish game of tip and run with an eight thousand ton avalanche suddenly run amok.

The Second Mate shook his head as if he couldn't really believe it was all happening – which made two of us. I snapped, 'Get everyone on deck, Barney . . . except the Chief.

I need him below for manœuvring. *Move*, laddie!'

Tanker said lugubriously, 'I'm gettin' bloody fed-up, I know that.'

I grinned at him nervously, I couldn't help it. And anyway, it was all building up so quickly that the only sensation I was really aware of was an almost philosophical acceptance of the *Sarikamis*'s inconsistency. Like a psychiatrist with an unbalanced patient. A homicidal one.

'Maybe we were better off aboard the *Vespasian* after all, huh? At least the only way *she* could go was straight bloody down!'

John called from the wing. He sounded as calm as a man remarking on the weather. 'She's steadied on course. And she is coming straight for us, Peter.'

Baffled resignation there too. I started to get the ridiculous feeling that, if the *Sarikamis* had suddenly sprouted wings and taken off over our heads we'd just have watched with detached interest.

Less than two hundred yards off now. Her speed maybe eight knots, pushing up to nine. Added to ours it gave a closing velocity of around twenty-two, twenty-three miles per hour. It wasn't very fast. Not until you remember that ships turn slowly too, even small ones like *Tactician* with no twin screws to help her round.

It meant I had to outguess an already established master of illogical action. I could either turn to port, or to starboard. I wouldn't get a second attempt.

We had a precise, fifty-fifty chance. And if I was wrong this time, the *Sarikamis* would just keep on going over us as if we weren't there at all. Tumbling and rolling us under just before she rode up on top of us and smeared John and Tanker and all the rest of our complement into oblivion.

She would turn once, and we would turn once. It was a simple straightforward spin of the coin.

I so desperately wanted to be right. Because, if I wasn't then I would never know one terribly important thing.

'*Why?*'

And then she was looming over us with the high, rust-scarred bow blanking off everything but the swelling blister of broken water pushing ahead of her, and the waves smashing excitedly into her flanks, slightly more forcefully along her weather side . . . but there wasn't any more time to think about anything except staying alive for another sixty seconds.

Or dying within fifty . . .

Eyes glued to the round of her stem, watching calculatingly for the slightest movement, the very first indication that she was veering off-centre . . . Tanker behind me, stolidly holding our course like a farm hand in a ploughing competition on the end of a die-straight, closing furrow . . . John through the open door, standing very erect and still . . . The beat of our own screw transmitting up through *Tactician*'s length to reveal itself in rattling window frames and the steady, ceramic chink of unheeded mugs on the chart table . . .

And suddenly she was swinging . . . Oh the clever bastard! He'd really got me figured . . . anticipating that, as a single screw ship, the odds were that I'd use the thrust of my prop to help me turn tighter to starboard . . . so *Sarikamis* had started to veer to her port hand in readiness . . . to meet us almost head on . . . !

I screamed, '*Port*, Tanker! Hard a port . . . !'

And waited. The coin was sparkling in the air and we were committed.

It seemed to spin for a very long time.

Barney Slough's tautly pitched bellow from aft. 'Hold onnnn*nnnn*!'

The rushing, battering roar of fast-moving water drowning the throb of *Tactician*'s engine. A crazily sliding wall of black moving sideways across the bridge windows and that great blister of sea climbing up and over our forward bulwarks to rage aft in a flood of indescribable violence.

John running frantically for the door, naked fear in his eyes now because he'd suddenly realised that if we listed only a few more degrees to starboard he'd go down between the two ships, all ready pre-wrapped in the torn-away shroud of our bridge wing.

The thunder of racing diesels above even the torrential sound of the sea. But they weren't our engines, this time. They were the echoes from the *Sarikamis*, projecting through her steel sides so close we could almost imagine we were in there alongside her own crewmen ...

I'm hanging on to the binnacle, feeling the ship rolling to port now, shying away from the giant in terror. Tanker still straddle-legged behind the wheel with a look of sheer bloody hatred fighting with the concentration in his features . . . The inclinometer lying over to twenty . . . thirty . . . thirty-five degr . . . !

Our stern suddenly swinging hard . . . *inwards*! Attracted towards the bulk of the freighter as our bows are forced out and away from her careering path ..

'Meet her! For Christ's sakes *meet* her, Bosunnnnnn!'

A shattering, scraping shriek from aft, with the tug rearing in agony. A distant voice screaming 'Wullie! Oh Jesus but will ye look at Wullie's arm ...'

And then it was all over!

The *Sarikamis* had gone.

But she didn't go very far away.

It seemed very quiet, all of a sudden.

John tentatively eased his grip on the door frame and muttered shakily, 'Oh lord but that was close.'

I was trembling too. I snapped savagely, 'Where's that homicidal bastard got to, an' who's been hurt on the after deck?'

'Willie Thompson, it must've been!' Tanker's face was black with rage. 'That was McKay yelling an' Thompson's his mate . . . Christ but I'd like to meet that bat-blind soddin' skipper again up a dark . . . !'

'You won't have to wait 'til it's dark, dammit! That was a

deliberate attempt to ram us, Tanker. They'll try again and again, while all we can do is bloody dodge and run!'

John said grimly, 'They're turning now, about half a mile inshore and dead astern.'

I tumbled out to the wing and looked anxiously aft. There didn't seem to be a lot of damage to our starboard quarter though several of the seamen were bending over someone lying on the deck. But the *Sarikamis* was my immediate problem right now — or there wouldn't be any deck left to lie on.

John wiped a hand across his face. It came away glistening but I don't know whether it was sweat, rain or spray. 'Maybe it was an accident,' he said unconvincingly. 'Maybe they just lost their bearings.'

I looked at him grimly. 'Do you really think they did? And anyway . . .' I couldn't resist a spiteful jibe, '. . . anyway, didn't it occur to you to wonder *who* the hell was trying to steamroller us. To look at the name of the bloody ship?'

He glared back irritably. 'I had other things on my mind. And I gave *you* the binoculars, remember?'

I looked quickly over his shoulder. She was well astern by now and still turning hard away from the shore. We had, maybe, ten minutes before she could present another threat.

And then she would kill us. And if she didn't, then she would the next time. Or the next. She had to, now. Or there would be too many questions to answer.

I stared back at John, feeling a bit guilty and knowing it wasn't the time for falling out. I said, 'Sorry, John. But that ship over there — she's the *Sarikamis*!'

He didn't look surprised, just more irritated. 'Oh, forget about your non-existent casualties for God's sake! It's that bastard who's out to sink us I'm worried about right now.'

Then he saw the look on my face and blinked hard. I nodded and gave him a lovely smile. 'That's right, Johnny boy. Your bastard and my casualty — they're one and the same . . . the good ship *Sarikamis*! Except she's about three hours late in getting herself wrecked like she . . . !'

I stopped dead.

Wrecked!

John's face was white with disbelief – the news about the *Sarikamis* was enough to shatter anyone, I could vouch for that personally – but maybe the way I took off and sprinted crazily through the open wheelhouse didn't do a hell of a lot to calm his overstrung nerves either.

I yelled 'Binoculars! Where's those bloody binoc . . . !'

Tanker still looked fit to kill someone. Slowly. And preferably a Turkish captain, though he didn't seem too fussy and, anyway, he didn't know about *that* particular piece of the jigsaw puzzle yet, either.

He growled, 'On the window ledge where you left 'em! An' when are we goin' to . . . !'

I didn't hear the rest of his no-doubt sanguinary ambition. I was already out on the port wing with the binoculars clamping up to my eyes. And a detailed memory of a recently studied chart in my mind.

Just in perfect time. I suppose it was quite a relief really. After what had just happened.

To watch a seven hundred foot long enigma called the *Sarikamis* doing exactly as she'd promised, three hours before.

By piling herself monstrously aground.

And precisely in the middle of my Scab Rocks.

CHAPTER FIVE

Not even John Templeton could conceal the fact that he considered it all a bit poetic and appropriate – the way the Turk had over-shot *Tactician* to run herself hard aground instead.

Before they'd had time to ring her still uselessly threshing propellers to 'Stop' he'd come up behind me, taken one terribly satisfied glance over my shoulder, and murmured cynically, 'Well at least we'll soon know the answers to a few very pertinent questions. Eh, Peter old son?'

Poor John. I suppose he'd even thought, for a little while longer, that our luck had finally changed for the better.

For instance the way the freighter was aground. At first sight she looked good, very good indeed. Quite challenging, in fact.

To a salvage crew, anyway.

Rather like a once beautiful woman might, after having been hurled through a Triplex windscreen – when seen through the eyes of a cosmetic surgeon.

Because the *Sarikamis* hadn't been able to work up to a really self-destructive speed before she'd hit the Scab. Through the binoculars she only appeared to be fast for roughly one quarter of her length abaft the bow. This meant that – presenting her stern to the seas as she did – there was a reasonable chance of her staying that way and not broaching to. If that did happen, then the substantial swell would pound her broadside-on against the reef and into a total loss within hours.

In other words, she was perfectly safe for the time being. And so was anyone remaining aboard her as long as they kept to the fore part of the casualty, avoiding the heavy seas which were already sweeping her after decks as an unmistakable warning to anyone trying to leave before the gale moderated.

Yet at that precise moment something happened, something which seemed so utterly beyond the reasoning of even the most irresponsibly inadequate seaman, that we could only assume we were witnessing one more incomprehensible twist in that excess of madness which appeared to have taken possession of the *Sarikamis*.

Suicidal at first. Then homicidal — but now, criminally imbecilic!

I'd watched her hit, then I'd lowered the binoculars and turned to John with a grin on my face like the Cheshire Cat from *Alice*.

'We're in business, mate,' I said, still not really believing it. 'And right now I don't give a damn how or why she got there. All I know is her owners'll be bloody glad to pay up if we can get her off again pretty damn quick.'

John looked at me doubtfully. 'You really think so?'

'Yeah . . . !' Then I saw what he meant and shrugged. 'You mean they may have actually arranged for her to run ashore. A coffin ship, huh?'

He shrugged back. '*Somebody* did! We've not been watching a crazy man, Peter. Whoever's in command of the *Sarikamis* is an icy cold, calculating operator.'

'He's a killer . . . or as near being one as dammit!' I glanced over to where the ship snuggled almost chummily into the welter of foam marking the Scab. Her engines were at stop now but there was still white water smashing into her exposed stern, flinging high in the air to hang temporarily suspended above her mast trucks.

Maybe John was right. Maybe it was an insurance fraud — establish a total constructive loss, over-price the cargo . . . and hit the jackpot when the claim's paid up! But it still didn't sound quite feasible. Something still didn't fit the jigsaw. The *Sarikamis* herself, for a start. A virtually new ship — no possibility there of over-valuing. Which made John's theory a bit like burning real money in exchange for counterfeit.

And the way she had originally been steaming full ahead into those creepy cliffs up near Ras oum Achiche – anyone doing that deliberately had to be desperate to sink her for a lot more than any crooked owners would be offering as blood money. Whoever drove her like that was a man with a great deal at stake.

Or a very frightened one?

Which made me start wondering why she'd suddenly hauled clear in those last, frantic moments? And if the reason was anything to do with that briefly imagined struggle up there on her bridge . . . ? Then there was that Mayday we'd picked up on the VHF before she was even fifty miles from the place where she'd finally come to grief . . . ?

I deliberately shut the questions from my mind. I was a salvage man, not a detective. And, more to the point, I was also a nearly bankrupt salvage man. Like John.

In other words *we* were desperate, too. Just like the anonymous man on that ship over there. We didn't need to know the reasons why – we needed the salvage award on the *Sarikamis* instead. To buy back a dream we were so near to losing.

The Templeton Ross Towing Company couldn't afford the luxury of official inquiries and delaying investigations. This was Algeria, where we could spend more time making endless statements than we could on saving the casualty. We needed time to do our job without police protection . . .

I frowned. What strange influence had made me think about that . . . ? About needing protection? Because the *Sarikamis* couldn't hurt us any more. Not now. Not helpless as she was on the Scab Rocks.

Could she . . . ?

I shivered involuntarily and the cold, uneasy fingers stroked the back of my neck again. I turned on John sharply. 'It doesn't matter a damn whether her owners want her salvaged or not. Her insurers will an' *that's* for bloody certain!'

Then our somnolent Chief Radio Operator came stumbling up the bridge ladder waving a signal pad like a man with the prize-winning ticket in the Irish Sweepstakes.

'We got it, Skipper! That distress call of yours . . . Boat called the . . . ah . . . *Sa-ree-kamiss*. And by God but she's not far from here, boys. Damn near blew my ears off when she . . . !'

His voice trailed off in bewilderment as I very gently led him out and turned him to face the ship sitting on top of a rock, so close now that we could have shouted to her on a quiet day.

I said nicely, 'Thank you, Mister Styles. Now how would you like to go back to bed, huh?'

He'd started to shuffle back down the ladder like a very dazed old man when a thought struck me. I called, 'How did that Mayday come in, Sparks? What frequency?'

He blinked. 'Five hundred! And twenty-one, eighty-two as well . . . W/T and radio telephone. Why?'

'Professional operator?'

'The keying was pro. Probably the same bloke making the voice transmission right after. Sounded foreign to me.'

I nodded. 'Turkish! But those last calls must have been made on her main equipment, right? No chance of her having anything that powerful on her bridge, say?'

He shook his head. 'Not unless she's the QE Two. So if I read you right, the chances are that your earlier call on VHF was made by another bloke . . . probably direct from her bridge set like you thought.'

Which was precisely what I wanted to know. It meant that someone — most likely one of the *Sarikamis*'s deck officers — had jumped the gun in anticipation of a wrecking which he *knew* was going to happen. The proper distress call had come at the right time, from her normal operator, still quite possibly unaware that anything irregular was happening until just before she hit . . .

So why had our apparently prophetic navigator made that

earlier VHF call at all . . . unless he wanted to make damned sure someone within steaming distance was waiting to give assistance right away?

Yet why should he then try and *sink* his lifeboat when he'd gone to all that risk to arrange its presence in the first place . . . ?

I didn't feel too confused this time. Maybe I was just getting used to the crazy world of the *Sarikamis.*

Until John gasped disbelievingly, 'Peter! The boats. They're lowering her boats in that surf f'r . . . The bloody fools are abandoning ship!'

And the real horror of the Scab Rocks disaster was about to commence.

The Second Mate hauled himself to the top of the ladder and snarled grimly, 'Thompson's arm! Smashed in two, maybe three places. He needs a surgeon bad, Skip . . . !'

I swung round on him. 'Get him down to the medical room, Barney. Give him morphine then break out all the spare blankets you can find. And have the cook organise hot soup and coffee . . .'

I hesitated, hardly taking my eyes off the bright orange blob which was the first of the *Sarikamis*'s boats inching seawards from her davits. '. . . there could be a lot like Thompson, Barney. Those stupid bastards are abandoning.'

His eyes followed mine but the savage expression didn't change one bit. 'Yeah? So I'll tell Willie Thompson and see if it makes him feel any better – when they amputate his left hand!'

John started to say quietly, 'Easy, Barney. Most of the *Sarikamis* crew wouldn't even have known about . . . !' but the Second Mate spun on his heel and went clattering down the ladder again. John didn't call him back but I could see the anger in his eyes at the snub. We were all getting a bit nervy though – and we all knew there wasn't much of a future in the salvage business for a one-armed deck hand.

I said quickly, 'I'll take us in as close as I dare, not that it'll be much help to them.'

He nodded, the irritation fading. John knew what I meant – that the critical part of getting away from the *Sarikamis* was going to be in surviving that first hundred yards of rampaging water running seawards from her stern.

Her lifeboats were facing forward – towards the shore. But they couldn't take the easy route because less than fifty yards ahead of their bows lay the white-laced razor edges of the Scab, revealing themselves only occasionally as tons of roaring water atomised into hanging spume before hurling towards them again with indescribable force.

Her boats would have to clear the stranded ship without losing any of that impossibly narrow margin – which meant they would have to sheer broadside-on to breakers maybe fifteen feet high. And before the frantic survivors had a hope in hell of bringing their boats' bows round into the sea those opaque walls of vertical water would already be hanging over their heads, curving downwards in crumbling, thundering collapse, rolling and pulverising bits of already dead men and oars and thwarts and tattered orange alloy skin shorewards.

And back on to the very reef they were trying so hopelessly to claw clear of.

It would be sheer bloody suicide.

Except that I knew it wasn't – that it would be plain, unvarnished murder instead!

Because there were fifty or sixty men making up the crew of the *Sarikamis*. And fifty or sixty men don't just decide to run themselves aground at eighteen knots. Which, in turn, suggested that very few of them could have known about the stranding before it had actually happened – that they were simply victims of circumstance.

And as such they would still be carrying out orders given by their superior officers – even when they must have realised there was something terribly wrong with the events leading up to the stranding. It is a very resolute seaman who ignores an order to abandon ship without knowing all the odds against his surviving by staying on board. He's just one of a crowd, the herd instinct has taken over, and the shock and panic dictate his actions from that moment on.

'The men on the bridge know best. She's goin' to blow. Break up – Jesus, she's going to *capsize* . . . ! So do what you're told, laddie, or take your bloody chances all alone when the bitch goes down . . . !'

Someone on that anguished ship was about to kill half a hundred men. Quite coldly, and with the utmost deliberation!

Then the first boat hit the water, and all we could do was cruise off-shore. And watch.

Only two boats left her altogether – that first orange shape upended twenty feet above the sea when her after falls parted, spilling maybe fifteen men into the white foam immediately and taking the other six demented flies clinging to it down on top of their disgorged shipmates a minute later, when the bow falls couldn't stand the strain any longer.

And *that* was a strange thing too, because with fairly new ships and modern davits, wire ropes don't fail as often as many people imagine . . .

Though, as Tanker would have said – it didn't really make very much difference.

The second lifeboat hit with a great splash, neatly releasing on the crest of a roller and with all her crewmen securely seated and waiting – no signs of panic there anyway. Terror maybe, and apprehension, but none of the fatal indications of the crazed hysteria which could kill them before they'd even started to pull away.

Her engine must have been running before she reached the water as, with tiller hard over towards the sheer sides of the *Sarikamis*, she immediately swung away in a wide bucketing curve with the high, whispering swell blanking her completely from sight one moment until, almost incredibly, a brightly coloured sliver clambered above the next crest to show she was still afloat and under control.

I heard myself whispering tightly, 'By God, John, but there's at least one proper seaman aboard that floating lunatic asylum.'

John turned away quickly, hope showing in his eyes. 'I'll get aft. See that we're ready to . . . !'

Then the orange stick came up over the next wave top, only it looked a bit different this time because there seeemed to be too much orange and not enough men showing, and I realised with a surge of nausea that I was looking at the bottom of an already empty lifeboat so I allowed the binoculars to drop against my chest and said bitterly, 'Why bother. They aren't in any hurry now. Not any more.'

I left him standing out on the wing and strode into the wheelhouse. Tanker's eyes met mine and I didn't want him to know I just couldn't stand and watch men dying any longer, so I snarled, 'Bring her round to the east, Bosun. We'll run down past the tail of the reef and come back inshore towards the beach . . . Just in case any of them survive long enough to reach it.'

John appeared in the doorway. He said quietly, 'The third boat . . . they never even made it away from the ship . . .'

Then he hesitated for a moment. When he spoke again it seemed to underline more graphically than anything else how close we'd come to that point where an excess of horror numbs conventional priorities.

'. . . but it's stopped raining,' he added encouragingly. 'It's going to be a nice day !'

The sun came out just after midday. Within half an hour the whole bay was shimmering under a heat haze which reflected back from the white sands with an excruciating glare. To the east we could still see the cliffs running out towards Bougaroni, though they didn't seem so dangerous now, or threatening. Inshore, beyond the beach, the Algerian landscape sloped gently away in an Eden-like confusion of palm and oleander.

Westwards lay Djidjelli and the corkscrewing clifftop highway of the *Corniche d'Or*. Both John and I knew that area well – the Navy had introduced us to it when they sent us out to work on the scatter of wrecks surrounding Bejaia. They called it Bougie in those days, before Algeria was a place for Algerians and France became a dirty word, and Bougie had been one of the main assembly anchorages for east-bound convoys during the war. And in the peace which followed, a place of skeletons and shattered hulls, and memories.

Right in front of us sat the good ship *Sarikamis*, snuggled on to the Scab Rocks as neatly – and almost as safely – as in any dry dock. She even looked neat as a pin, as if nothing had ever happened to her, with only the hanging lifeboat falls and the empty davits along her port side to prove she'd ever had a crew aboard at all.

She was a salvage man's dream of a stranded casualty.

Like John had said – it was going to be a nice day.

Except for the tidying-up.

We'd sent a message to the Algerian authorities saying that we had picked up the *Sarikamis* Mayday – the proper one – and that we were standing by the casualty. We also asked for assistance from the medical and sanitary organisations. We made that bit an urgent request because it gets very hot in North Africa, even on a December day.

We didn't suggest that anything other than a rather over-hasty and tragically ill-advised abandonment had occurred. John hadn't wanted to conceal anything but I finally convinced him that we couldn't afford to invite the inevitable delays a Middle Eastern investigation would mean. Not right then, anyway. Not until after we'd re-floated the *Sarikamis* and filed our salvage claim.

Until then she would be just another wreck. Another

unfortunate sacrifice to the sinister winds and tide-rips west of Ras oum Achiche, another struggle between the age old sea and the crazy infidel salvors. Who wins is already written – it is the Will of Allah.

And by then *Tactician* had anchored neatly between the Scab and the shore. It was still too rough, too dangerous even for us to attempt to board that silent, enigmatic ship, but we still had one more obligation to fulfil anyway – one humane duty before we could surrender fully to commercialism.

So we went for a stroll. Along the beach.

John didn't go. I don't think either of us wanted to, and someone had to stay and contact the *Sarikamis*'s owners to secure an agreement on salvage anyway and John was the business end of the partnership.

As the wreck was presumably abandoned the mere fact that we were about to board her ensured our right to claim salvage – if we managed to wrest her from the Scab's jealous clutches, that was – but a standard form of open contract, negotiated in advance with her owners on the traditional 'No cure – no pay' basis, would smooth our path considerably when it came to the final tussle over percentages and values.

Either way, Templeton Ross Towing were undoubtedly back in business. I remember looking back at the *Sarikamis* as the inflatable roared ashore, and thinking, 'Please God. Please make that bloody awful sea die down. And let us find she's not too badly holed when you do allow us to go on board . . .'

I did also wonder how keen Messrs Hazar, Melen and Company would be to encourage us to save her, if John had been right about her being an insurance fraud – and how in God's name, if she *was* a coffin ship, they had managed to arrange the suicide of the very man or men responsible for her grounding.

How much do you have to pay a man to kill himself?

I knew then that I could never rest until I'd solved the

horrible mystery lying so placidly now on the teeth of the Scab . . . and then the Avon grounded in a waterborne flurry of white, clouding sand, and we splashed ashore to search hopelessly among the things washed up on that silver North African beach.

Things like a corpse without a head, and a head without a corpse. And an arm still attached to something else and a gaggle of bobbing, inflated creatures swirling ghoulishly in and out of the tide lap.

And other monstrosities which were pieces of men once, before the sea and the rocks of the Scab had ravaged them. All mixed up in a flotsam purée of shattered planking and punctured buoyancy tanks and splintered lengths of oar.

There was a cap and part of a sea boot, and someone's suitcase with Turkish lettering still distinguishable in the corner of it. And a sinuously floating nylon warp with one end made fast to a green canvas sea-anchor and the other coiled untidily around what had been a radio operator in the Turkish merchant navy.

He was still clutching something small against his chest. We carried him ashore and laid him gently on the sand, and Tanker ever so carefully pulled the poor, mutilated arm away to reveal what must have been the most precious possession in that dark-skinned seaman's existence.

It was a kitten. A tiny, bedraggled little ball of fluff which looked up at us with great big almond eyes – and then calmly started to lick itself all over as though there wasn't anything special at all in being the sole survivor of a massacre.

McKay doubled over, retching, and was sick in the water. The other men pretended not to see, which wasn't a very good idea either because wherever else they looked they learnt more about the awful things that water and submerged rocks can do to a man.

I began to walk back along the tide line, thinking about the drowned radio officer and wondering if he could have told us any more than we already knew about the loss of the Sari-

kamis, and wondering which of those shapeless lumps of meat back there was a murderer. And, presumably, a self-destructive lunatic as well.

Tanker caught up with me, carrying the kitten in one horny, protective paw. He fell in step and, for a few paces, we walked in silence towards the inflatable. Then he said quietly, 'We'll bring those . . . the bodies ashore, Skipper. Maybe the local Arabs'll be here to do the rest, eh?'

He pronounced it *Aye-rabs*. It's funny how you notice small things, even when you feel . . . I frowned. I'd never really analysed my reactions up to then but, when I did, I found I was only conscious of one major emotion. And that realisation gave me an involuntary surge of shock.

Because underlying all the conflicting passions of horror at what had happened, and obsessive determination to find out why – and maybe just a little bit of gratitude for this last chance to save our dream – I was aware of one unsettling, and utterly inexplicable sensation.

I realised I was still very, very apprehensive indeed!

I stopped, staring seawards to where that great ship waited so passively for us to attempt to take her. Tanker halted too, fondling the kitten with absent tenderness, and I could feel him watching me curiously, waiting for me to say something.

So I muttered, without any real conviction at all, 'Well, Tanker. We've got our Big One, just like we've always wanted. In pretty good shape and without a damned soul aboard to make things awkward . . .'

But we were looking at a ship called the *Sarikamis*. So we weren't really surprised even then when a signal lamp started flashing, quite emphatically, from her bridge!

CHAPTER SIX

Though it was disconcerting, to say the least. To find there were still survivors remaining aboard the *Sarikamis*.

It also occurred to me to wonder, while Tanker gunned the Avon in a crazily skittering dash back to *Tactician*, just why whoever was belatedly using that Aldis had decided to wait for over three hours after the rest of her crew had abandoned before trying to contact us.

But I didn't work too hard on the possible answers. Too many theories had already been demolished right after conception, as soon as the *Sarikamis* affair had taken yet another lunatic twist in the sequence of events.

Though this current revelation did afford me one satisfying glimmer of anticipation. In that one critical factor holding the key to the mystery was certain to be solved as soon as we boarded the enigmatic Turkish puzzle sitting on top of the Scab – when the identity of the person who'd sacrificed all those lives was finally revealed.

And, presumably, the killer in person. It seemed a pretty safe bet, even against the current odds, that he would be among those still remaining safely and securely on board the *Sarikamis*.

But that possibility, in its turn, presented a chilling alternative – because where we had originally assumed we were watching the final act of madness by a self-destructive maniac, we were now about to come face to face with a still very much alive mass murderer.

And when someone had already attained such heights of homicidal accomplishment, presumably he doesn't have too many reservations about adding to his final total.

Especially when we were about to try and salvage a ship

which *he* had just risked his own neck in attempting to sink . . .

. . . and then the inflatable had slammed against *Tactician*'s ladder and John had leapt aboard, leaving Barney Slough on her bridge to follow us at a more leisurely pace round the tail of the reef.

Tanker opened out the big Mercury immediately and I felt the Avon riding up on the plane with the spray sheeting out like great white wings on each side. I'd just turned to John, who was hanging on with a pleased look all over his face, and started to ask him if he'd got anywhere with the salvage contract when – like a bolt from the blue – what little was left of my satisfied glow evaporated completely, and the sick fear came back with stunning impact.

When I realised that, not only had we got ourselves a highly competent killer for company, but that we couldn't even *tell* anyone about it.

Not now.

Not unless John and I wanted to spend so long inside a Middle Eastern jail that the *Sarikamis* would have enough time to rust away, never mind break up, before we finally came out as free men.

Because I had convinced John that no useful purpose would be served by inviting official investigation into the *Sarikamis* deaths. That whoever was responsible was gone too, drowned and beyond the reach of justice along with all those other poor bloody Turkish sailormen.

So when we had informed the Algerian authorities that we were in the vicinity of, and standing by the casualty, we'd also conveniently forgotten to mention our having actually been witnesses of the whole affair, including that earlier attempt to destroy herself against the cliffs below Ras oum Achiche. And her unsuccessful ramming of our own vessel.

And those were the two vital events which altered the reasons for the wrecking of the *Sarikamis* from 'accidental' to 'deliberate'. And turned manslaughter by incompetent seamanship into murder. Premeditated murder.

It meant that my anxiety to save a dream by concealing what I'd originally considered as a no-longer-useful part of the truth, had also unwittingly involved us as accessories.

Accessories after the fact, certainly.

But the fact was still . . . Mass Murder!

There were five men waiting for me altogether, standing round the head of the pilot ladder as I raised my eyes above the level of the after bulwarks for my first view along the decks of the Motor Ship *Sarikamis*.

The couple hovering uncertainly in the background were obviously Turkish deck- or engine-room hands. Darkly handsome men with fierce moustaches and dressed in those washed-out denim jeans which are Levi's standard rig for international seamen.

Number three was Turkish as well. A slim, nervous-looking kid who didn't seem to be able to make up his mind whether he was pleased or disconcerted to see me. He wore an oil-stained reefer jacket which I supposed made him some kind of officer, though judging by the way his hands twitched I guessed he would be about as much use in a disaster as a ten foot stepladder.

The last two members of the welcoming committee were different. Quite a lot different.

One was fat. Incredibly, enormously fat – yet still revealing a trace of hardness which seemed strangely at odds with his gross frame. He was obviously a European, I could see that much in the rather too pink skin showing through the open vee of his collar – but maybe I wouldn't want to work with my shirt off either, not if I had an obesity problem like him.

Then there was his hair, or to be more accurate the faint colourwash of jet black bristle which seemed to crown the powerfully shaped head like a skullcap. His hair and the eyes below it – they were the things which registered first in my mind. This mammoth survivor of the *Sarikamis* grounding had

the English language they could understand. The young kid in the stained reefer still looked more scared than aggressive though, almost on the verge of tears in fact, and I made a mental note that screwing information from him could well be our easiest solution.

But later. And discreetly. When nobody was around to back him up.

John said calmly, 'I should advise you that your owners, Hazar, Melen and Company, have just awarded us the contract to salvage this ship. Lloyd's Open Form of Agreement . . . We propose to start work immediately.'

I stared at him, admiration struggling with the anger inside me. During that hectic trip over in the Avon I'd been so wrapped up in the mess I'd talked us into that I hadn't given John the chance to explain the pleased look on his face.

So we really were in business, set up by John through direct radio contact with the *Sarikamis* owners, and in record time. And there was another interesting sidelight from this new information – that as Messrs Hazar Whatnot had agreed so promptly, it also seemed to put the last nail firmly in the lid of the coffin ship fraud theory for once and for all.

Beside Tilsley I noticed Fat Boy watching through those pudding swamped eyes, and wondered exactly what he was thinking. And just who he was anyway, and why the presence of such a comically gross cartoon of a human being should make me feel so uneasy.

The *Sarikamis*'s Mate didn't seem all that pleased at the news. But that could only be expected if he was involved with the wrecking attempts. He raised one eyebrow at John in interrogation. 'And exactly when did you contact my owners, Mister Templeton? Before or after you realised there were still members of the original crew on board this ship?'

I knew what he meant. An abandoned vessel is anybody's prize, whereas one still under command is a very different thing. But John was ready for him.

'Before! But it doesn't really make any difference, Tilsley . . .' He glanced meaningfully aft to where the swell still threw great spinners of spume above the *Sarikamis*'s poop deckhousing. '. . . Not unless you're prepared to advise them that a salvage team isn't necessary, and that you are able to refloat her yourself. And to justify your decision to the insurer's assessors when they arrive.'

Tilsley still didn't like it, I could see that in his face. But he was only the Chief Officer – the final decision would be left to the casualty's Master, if he was still aboard. Otherwise it was a perfectly understandable reaction. No crewman likes moving over to make room for the salvage men.

But no wrecker does, either.

I stared pointedly at Tilsley's triple-braided sleeve. 'Maybe we're discussing the salvage question with the wrong man, Peter. Captains wear four rings in anyone's navy.'

Tilsley just stared right back at the anonymous, frayed sleeves of my once-white sea jersey and looked all surprised. '*Do* they . . . ah . . . was it *Captain* Ross? Or just plain Mister?'

I glared angrily at him for a moment, feeling a growing sense of injustice because if anyone should be disconcerted aboard the *Sarikamis* it was Tilsley, certainly not me. Unless, of course, he didn't have anything to feel guilty about.

John asked hurriedly, 'And exactly who *is* left aboard, Tilsley?'

The Mate took a last, hard glance at me then turned towards the young, worried looking Turkish kid. 'Third Officer Rifat Burak . . .'

Burak jumped as though Tilsley had suddenly shouted '*Boo!*' but the Englishman's thumb was already pointing towards the two impassive seamen in the Levi's and identical moustaches. '. . . The Brothers Mentese – Ahmet and Nihat. Ordinary seamen. Good boys but a little slow on the uptake sometimes . . .'

John glanced meaningfully towards the beach where the rest of the *Sarikamis* crew went in and out with the tide. 'But not always, eh Mister?'

Tilsley hesitated, looking bitter. 'You think we should be over there too, don't you, Templeton? So why the hell don't you say it.'

I caught sight of the fat man. He was just standing there, watching us. Almost as though he was waiting for something . . . or perhaps just hoping? Then John shrugged, it was his turn to be icy cold. 'I might yet, Mister. I don't like being deliberately run down – but please carry on with the introductions first.'

I watched bleakly. The formality was so bizarre – like having a cabaret act in the middle of a funeral. But I wanted to find out just what slot Fat Boy so amply filled among the stranded ship's complement too. Tilsley gave an imperceptible shrug and gestured.

'Bosun of the *Sarikamis* . . . Karl Lenz!'

I said, 'Lenz. You a German then?' I was genuinely surprised, somehow I'd imagined Lenz as being a bigger fish in this particular pond and, anyway, merchant navy petty officers are usually of the same nationality as the hands. Not that it was all that odd – not compared to the rest of the *Sarikamis* enigma.

Maybe the gargantuan matelot mistook my meaning. Either way he just stared calculatingly at me for a moment until, all of a sudden, the folds of flesh around the piggy eyes creased even more as that curious sailorman's face bloomed into a totally unexpected grin.

But it wasn't a friendly smile. Somehow it held more of a promise than a reaction. Even the chuckle which went with it sounded vaguely threatening. 'The war is over, *Kapitan* Ross. Now we are all good friends, *hein*?'

I didn't smile back. 'Let's just say the war is over, *Herr* Lenz.'

Tilsley swung on me. That trace of bitter accusation was still there in his voice. 'I would suggest you find out who *was* responsible for this morning's affair before you make snide remarks to Lenz or anyone else, Ross!'

I said carefully, 'All right, Mister. Then who *did* give the order to abandon?'

The grey eyes never flickered. 'The master – Captain Sevket Koroglu . . . Koroglu also drove her in towards Ras oum Achiche, Captain Ross. *And* attempted to run your ship down after he'd failed. These men are all witnesses . . .'

He hesitated as the *Sarikamis* shuddered and the scream of tortured metal echoed from forward. '. . . D'you really want the story now? About what happened this morning?'

Damn right I did. But there wasn't time. That gut-wrenching screech from below told me the ship had already started to work against the reef. Every minute lost would be sixty seconds nearer to the final break up of both her and our dream . . . I glanced anxiously over to John. He was still watching Tilsley's face closely and I wondered whether he believed him or not because, to me, the Mate was either genuinely bewildered or a superlatively cool and convincing liar. Quite honestly I just didn't know.

Another big roller lifted her stern and the ship lurched again. John bit his lip and said quietly, 'Not at present, Tilsley. Not except for one thing . . . where is Captain Koroglu now, Mister?'

The Chief Officer of the *Sarikamis* turned and looked towards the shore. *Tactician*'s beach party were still moving along the tide line half a mile away but from this distance you couldn't really see what they were fishing for. Further inshore, still masked by the oleander trees, a cloud of rising sand heralded the arrival of the first Algerian ambulances. Not that there was any hurry any more.

Tilsley's face was tight. I also noticed, with a faint shock of surprise, that the young Turkish Third Officer standing beside him really was crying now, just before the Englishman gestured towards the glare from the silver sand on the other side of the Scab.

'Over there somewhere, I suppose. The Captain was in the

first boat to leave, Mister Templeton . . . I saw him being crushed to death when her falls carried away!'

He looked so much like a nice clean-cut seaman fighting a pent-up emotion which must, were he genuine, have been tearing at his nerves. I think that perhaps was the moment when I first felt a murmur of sympathy for Mike Tilsley. Anyone who'd watched in close up as his shipmates retched their last seconds of life away would carry a scar in their mind for the rest of their time on earth.

It was only a momentary twinge, though. Until it struck me that an assassin might look just like that as well — while claiming that his victim had actually committed suicide instead.

But there wasn't any immediate hurry to decide — in fact an instant confession could just be a bit embarrassing, in view of our present position with the authorities. Those sailors were dead and gone, the truth couldn't bring any of them back, and there were other priorities if we wanted to save the *Sarikamis*.

I almost convinced myself I was justified in thinking like that.

Almost.

It only occurred to me later, but the man standing behind Tilsley — Herr Bosun Karl Fat Boy Lenz — hadn't stopped grinning all the time we'd been talking.

Not even when the rest of us had been staring over towards thoses industrious fishermen on the flotsam-dappled beach.

CHAPTER SEVEN

Time would now be our most desperately restricted commodity.

Everything we wanted to do needed time. Time to survey the casualty, to take soundings around her stern, to carry out an underwater examination of the grip which the Scab had on her forward section. Time to transfer pumps from *Tactician* to reinforce the Turk's own discharge capacity – if only we could find even more time, and the resources, to repair the inevitable underwater damage she'd sustained in the first place.

We needed time to plan and calculate, to prepare for the final attempt to pull her off by shifting ballast and even cargo if necessary, in order to lighten the downward squeeze of her bows against the reef. There would be virtually no tide to help us for this was the Mediterranean, so every inch of freeboard gained forward would mean the physical transferring of tons of weight to her still spume-lashed after end.

Time had to be allocated to familiarising ourselves with the freighter's engine room, to running up her generators so that the salvage crews struggling overnight would have light and power, and to testing her main engines in order to use her own screws to help drag her clear. And a little time to eat and even less time to sleep . . .

And then there was time which would be swallowed voraciously by the sea itself, and turned against us as it moved the *Sarikamis* shudderingly back and forward, up and down against the teeth of the Scab, each fractional change of position enabling them to gnaw deeper and wider into the stricken ship's belly. And that same time which the sea's ally – the temporarily dormant westerly gale – would use to replenish its strength before once again screaming in to the fray.

We would lose time, John and I, in completing the ritualistic formalities with the marine surveyors and insurance assessors who would already be flying into this God-forsaken place in order to put a price on a grievously wounded patient. And with the Algerian authorities who were even then arriving on the beach in gaping, gesticulating knots and who – even when in ignorance of the real truth – would still be forced to ask some awkward questions because fifty or sixty men had died horribly, right after running into their own back yard.

And it would take time – a great deal of time perhaps – for us to find out more about Captain Sevket Koroglu, late of the Turkish Merchant Marine. And also why he had apparently decided to die, along with those fifty or sixty men under his command . . .

. . . *if* Captain Sevket Koroglu had been given any alternative in the first place. But the answer to that particular riddle lay with the tautly composed Chief Officer Tilsley and the strangely amused Herr Karl Lenz. And, of course, with the tearful kid with the tortured mind and maybe even with the blank-eyed Turkish Brothers Mentese.

Perhaps a tiny part of the answer still lay within the *Sarikamis* herself. Some clue, some indication at least of 'why'. But surely only the survivors could know the real truth about why this ship had indirectly killed most of her crewmen, or had Tilsley already told us as much as he knew when he accused a dead captain . . . ?

Had a mutilated cadaver now grounding sluggishly against a North African beach really been a killer? Or had he been merely another victim instead? We had to know. But it would take a lot of time to be sure and, until we were, those five oddly assorted suspects had every right to stay aboard and assist us in saving the ship for their owners.

Which meant that not only would Tilsley and company be

free to prowl at will among us, but that they would also be able to do anything they wanted without supervision. Because we were short of men too, as well as time, and we just couldn't afford the insurance of detailing watchers to watch the . . . watchers?

The snag was that, if any of our unwanted shipmates really were involved then he, or they, might possibly try to kill us too.

Because whoever was guilty had already proved himself very, very proficient indeed at the esoteric act of mass murder.

And liberally indiscriminate. In their selection of victims!

I'd turned away from the rail, and the beach, to find the *Sarikamis* men watching me closely, almost conspiratorially. Which could well figure, at that. But it still gave me a nervous twinge of unease, all the same.

Tilsley said calmly, 'I suppose I'd better stay aboard unless my owners want me back in Ankara to report. The ship's still my responsibility until then.'

Reaction precisely as anticipated. Looking on the bright side it at least meant that someone was conforming to my expectations, and even that made a change aboard this screwed-up wreck. It didn't mean a damn thing, though — maybe Tilsley's reasons for remaining weren't quite as he'd stated.

I said coldly, 'Please yourself! We'll arrange for the others to be flown out as distressed seamen as soon as . . . !'

'*Nein!*'

The harsh accent stopped me dead and I turned to see Lenz glaring at me through three or four purple-tinged folds of flesh. I reflected bitterly, 'You'd look more at home standing beside a human skin lampshade with a whip an' a bloody SS armband, you Teutonic . . .'

'This ship is not abandoned, *Kapitan* Rose . . .'

'Ross!' I snapped with little-boy peevishness.

Lenz shrugged to show me he couldn't have cared less if my parents had christened me Daisy. '. . . therefore I am still

Bosun according to her articles. And I too will stay aboard until my owners order otherwise. *Verstehen?*'

And I *verstehened* pretty good. If we wanted the *Sarikamis*, then we got Fat Boy and the Gieves' Dummy along with the rest of the package. I still tried, though. 'It's funny,' I grated heavily, 'but on all the ships I ever served aboard the Chief Officer was the one who gave the orders . . . or is it the heavy with the loudest mouth in your navy, Lenz?'

John said warningly, 'Easy, Peter . . . for now.'

The obscene eyes stared at me calculatingly for another few seconds then, abruptly, the German switched his gaze to Tilsley. I noticed that Tanker had moved quietly up behind the fat man during the brisk repartee, and he wore a look which suggested that the only thing he'd liked to have done more than save the ship was to punch Lenz right in the mouth. If he could find it.

Another thing I noticed – that the silent Brothers Mentese had moved in behind Tanker. And that one of them was casually paring his nails with the kind of knife you'd give to a brain surgeon for Christmas.

I think it was at that moment that I finally knew we'd involved ourselves – *I'd* involved us – in more than just a dubious salvage job. That there was a nightmarish quality about the situation which was trapping us deeper and deeper into the promise of violent things to come. And that the stench of death which hung over the *Sarikamis* wasn't only because of deeds now past, but also in anticipation of horrors yet unrevealed.

And it wasn't even as simple as 'Us' against 'Them' – the survivors. Because even as I watched I could feel the tension between Tilsley and the bloated creature before me, a fear and a mistrust so tangible I could almost taste it in the air. Until, incredibly, it was the so-self-possessed Chief Officer's eyes which dropped away in obvious defeat before he turned to me savagely.

'He stays, Ross! Lenz, Burak, the Brothers . . . they all

bloody stay an' be *damned* to . . . !'

He seemed to get a grip on himself and when he spoke again it was the smooth, competent, all-British merchant navy officer behind the mask. 'Right, Captain. We're in your hands. What do we do?'

I saw that Lenz was wearing a very satisfied look once again and that the Turks in the Levi's had gone back to looking placidly handsome and enigmatic so I thought it was pretty safe to tell him. 'Personally, Mister . . .' I enunciated quite clearly and emphatically. 'You can take your Turkish delights an' stu . . . !'

'You'll work, Tilsley . . . !' John's voice was very low and hard. 'By *God* but you'll work to save this ship! And you'll answer questions too, when we decide the time is right to ask them. And you, Herr Lenz – there's a lot of things I'd like to hear your version of . . . do *you verstehen*, this time.'

The grin on Fat Boy's face switched out like a fused light bulb. 'I do not answer questions from a *zweiter Güte* . . . ah . . . a second-rate salvage man, Templeton. Not from the hired help.'

'It's precisely because we're second-rate that you're even going to get the chance, Lenz. We need this salvage contract and that's why – so far – we've reported nothing other than the basic facts to the authorities. But one step out of line, Mister, and we tell the whole story of what happened this morning . . . and *then* you'll really find out what a Middle Eastern police interrogation is like!'

I heard a choking sob and swung round in time to see the young kid, Burak, doubled over and retching helplessly in the scuppers. Ignoring him I glanced quickly along the other faces in the row, searching anxiously for some clue, some indication of who might be rather less enthusiastic than the others to meet the Algerian Gendarmerie on a strictly professional basis.

It was a wasted effort. The two brothers still looked as though they were filling in time until their date with a belly dancer came up, while Tilsley, now apparently back to his original debonair self, seemed to be more interested in watching for Fat Boy's reaction too, rather than showing any individuality of his own.

John snapped impatiently, 'Well? Do we keep it in the family, or all paddle ashore for an intimate chat with the Arabs? It's your decision – for the moment!'

Tanker was so close to the fat Bosun now that they looked like two gladiators waiting for the bell. I wondered if this was the crunch, and whether Lenz would go for me or John first with those great white hands. Until, with typical *Sarikamis* inconsistency, the German's features blossomed into yet another of those outrageously disarming smiles.

'While I have nothing to conceal, Herr Templeton, I do have an aversion to the methods used by certain Middle Eastern *Polizeitruppen*. Even in some cases involving innocent persons. I feel sure your questions will be put in a much more . . . ah . . . civilised manner.'

I said heavily, 'Oh sure, Lenz. Nothing outside the Gestapo Manual of Interrogation . . . I bet it was Book Society Choice in your library club.'

'And you, Mister Tilsley?'

The Mate hesitated, still watching Lenz almost as if waiting for guidance. Then he shrugged. 'My responsibility is towards my owners, not towards the Algerian authorities. And I have never said I wouldn't tell you everything I could anyway, Templeton. Anytime you want.'

John nodded at the others. 'And them? We'll be talking to them too, Tilsley.'

Identical black eyes gazed back from the Brothers and I wondered again just how much English they could understand. Or would want to understand. Burak was dabbing shakily at his mouth with a soiled piece of cotton waste and there wasn't any way of telling whether he'd finally been sick with revulsion at what had happened to his crew mates or the thoughts of facing the Algerians. Or maybe both.

Tilsley nodded back but I still got the impression that it was really Lenz who was pulling the strings. 'They stay too.'

John glanced at me and I could see the uneasiness in his eyes, but there wasn't a damned thing we could do about it unless we were prepared, not only to give up any hope of re-floating the *Sarikamis*, but also to spending almost as long as Tilsley and crew in a game of Arabian Twenty Questions.

But salvaging a ship is a dangerous and highly intimate operation at any time. Like defusing an unexploded bomb. And in this case we were being forced to accept help with our particular bomb – but maybe from assistants with a homicidal leaning towards matches and hammers instead of safety.

'Very well! Just remember – you're neither welcome nor above suspicion until we are satisfied as to what really happened this morning . . .' John smiled for the first time, but there wasn't any warmth behind it. 'I'm sure Captain Ross will be able to suggest what you could do to help.'

This time I gave them my second favourite idea. Time was running out and there didn't seem any point in wasting it for the dubious satisfaction of being bloody-minded. 'Most of my crew-riggers, engineers, divers an' so on – will be working largely aboard this ship. I want them accommodated temporarily in the midships section, Tilsley . . . but I don't want them living amongst dead men's gear.'

I saw the Mate's lips tighten fractionally before he shrugged. 'I'll have all personal effects collected and removed from the cabins.'

'All except the Captain's. Leave Koroglu's quarters exactly as they are, Mister. And the rough deck and navigation logs – I want them too. Understand?'

I watched them as they turned away and wondered if we shouldn't start the quiz right then and have done with it, but the ship gave another scream from down below and I knew we couldn't leave her in the grip of the Scab much longer. Not without taking urgent action to relieve the strain on her forward section.

And we would have visitors very shortly, and they would have to be given priority even over the ship's safety, because this was Arab territory and there are certain ways to arrange things – and all of them slow.

I was pretty sure about one thing though. The curious Chief Officer Tilsley I couldn't fathom at all, and especially his tense relationship with the German . . . almost as if those three shiny rings should have been sewn around the fat arm instead – but I had Lenz established in my mind as a prominent member of the wrecking crew for certain! If any one of the *Sarikamis* survivors was candidate-elect for my Mass Murderer of the Year title, then it was Fat Boy.

I called after him as he climbed the centrecastle ladder, noticing as I did so the incredible agility of the gross frame. 'One thing, Lenz. Strictly as one second-class sailorman to another . . . what's your *real* reason for wanting to stay aboard this wreck? You're not the kind to be nervous of any tin-pot Bedouin police force an' you know it!'

For a few moments he stayed very still on the ladder. Then he turned to face me and I saw, with a surge of surprise, that for the first time since I'd met him there was no malice, and no trace of resentment, in the roly-poly features.

'Because I wish to help save this ship, *Kapitan* Ross.' His knuckles were white where they gripped the rails of the ladder. 'Because I want to see the *Sarikamis* salvaged very much indeed!'

But the eyes were cold, icy cold. And suddenly I felt even more confused, and even more frightened than ever before. And I didn't know why I should.

Because I really did believe he meant every word he said!

But it didn't put him on our side. I knew that too, without any doubt at all.

We had to work fast. To make decisions which might help to save the *Sarikamis* even before the inevitable delays of officialdom took place. And they were about to. Already we

78

could see the white flare of a fast launch battering towards us from the direction of Djidjelli.

Before it finally arrived Tanker had instructions to take two initial actions. The first was the essential task of laying the *Sarikamis*'s own anchors astern, from either quarter, in order to prevent the ship from swinging sideways against the Scab under the constant hammering of the swell. We all knew that if she did broach-to before we could secure her, then there was very little we could do to save her from becoming a total structural loss.

The second would be, to some extent, a retrograde step — we intended to sink the forward section of the ship.

Without the benefit of a preliminary survey it couldn't even be called a calculated risk — but somehow we had to minimise that awful, tearing movement caused as each successive swell lifted her stern, forcing the whole hull forward and downwards against the reef. And the only immediate solution was to use the rocks themselves as an anchor point — to bed the forefoot of the *Sarikamis* even deeper into the vice-like clutch of the Scab.

John said quietly, 'Tell the Chief — transfer all fuel and ballast forward, Tanker. Bed her down by the head.'

Tanker looked at him. 'She could break her back, you know that don't you? An' if we can't pump her out again she'll need a bloody railway engine to haul her off . . .'

'*SINK* her, dammit . . . !' I stared at John and saw his hands were trembling. So the *Sarikamis* was getting at him too, maybe even more than I'd realised. Then he seemed to get a grip on his nerves and sort of smiled at the Bosun.

'Sorry, Bose. Hobson's Choice. The Devil or the deep blue sea.'

Tanker's face broke into a grin and, just for a moment, I remembered that time so long ago when he'd laughed as a ship started to roll over on the two of us.

'I hates the bloody sea,' he said cheerfully. 'An' it could 'ave its compensations, goin' to the Devil.'

79

And then the officials arrived. And we started to lie away our last chance of protection within the law. Only John and I were involved from the *Tactician* complement but, had any of the others been questioned, then they would have given precisely the same negative replies. We all needed the *Sarikamis* for one reason or another – Barney and the Chief because the company meant something to them, Eddie Styles and Mike Tracey and most of the rest because she was worth a lot of money once clear of the Scab. And Tanker . . . ? Well, maybe he just needed the ship as an excuse. Because, apart from myself, he was the only one among us who had a very special personal feud with the Dragon.

The Algerians, smart men in military-style uniforms, were much more co-operative than we'd anticipated. They asked questions, certainly, but with impeccable correctness. They received answers, but not informative ones and, to our guilt-tinged relief, they didn't seem to give a damn either way. Or maybe we were seeing the fatalistic acceptance of the True Believers and anyway, they were only the local officials – the real probing would take place later, at the official inquiry into the *Sarikamis* tragedy.

After we'd saved her, and our dream. Or watched them both disintegrate so that it didn't matter any more.

Tilsley's crowd were questioned separately, in the saloon below the deserted bridge, but I knew that either way their stories would tally in every detail. And it did seem that, in the absence of any accusation from ourselves, this first visit was for the formality of recording – rather than querying – the manner in which their shipmates had died.

And by nightfall the Arabs had left, taking the injured Thompson with them and anxious, we suspected, to re-negotiate the hazards of the *Sarikamis* pilot ladder before the sea conditions deteriorated enough to invite the same fate for them as for those subjects of their paper work.

Perhaps they went away thinking that not only had Captain Sevket Koroglu been a very incompetent, but also a very stupid seaman. And maybe just a little confused too, because it had transpired that Allah had smiled favourably on two Christians like Tilsley and Lenz in preference to those of His own, still floating ashore on that sad beach inside the Scab.

I watched them go, sheering away into the dusk in a madly gyrating circle which showed that the sea was only resting temporarily, and listening absently to the throb of the *Sarikamis* auxiliaries transferring tons of fuel into her forward tanks. Then the cargo lamps slammed on, bathing the whole ship in an eerie glow which reflected outboard from the white caps of the rollers sweeping under her stern, and I felt the ship snuggling further into the reef and wondered tiredly if we'd ever get her off again.

John leaned over the rail beside me and watched the launch fade into the ring of darkness which was the world of the *Sarikamis* from now on. I said quietly, 'That's it then. She's all ours, Johnny. For better or for worse.'

He didn't answer because he didn't have to. His thoughts were mirrored in my own mind – that we were all alone now, with nobody to turn to for help.

Quite voluntarily we'd declared open season on ourselves, the salvage men.

All we had to do now was wait. To find out if the hunters were already among us.

We only had to wait until the next morning before we found part of the answer.

CHAPTER EIGHT

'MINES!' I yelled nervously, 'Whaddya mean . . . *mines?*'

John waved a cargo stowage plan impatiently at me. He'd been using it to calculate the extra weight factor required for transfer aft to raise the *Sarikamis*'s bows clear of the Scab. *If* we ever got as far as that, under the circumstances.

'Sea mines. She's loaded with general cargo – mainly tobacco, mohair, figs and raisins, cement, sugar . . .'

'The mines,' I snapped frustratedly. 'What about the *mines*, f'r . . .'

'Two hundred altogether. Royal Navy pattern contact mines. In transit from Ankara NATO Base to stores in the UK. Port of discharge, Liverpool.'

'Stowed where?'

'Right aft. Number six lower tween decks . . .' He shrugged, 'So it's a part-cargo of munitions. Not particularly unusual, and certainly no reason for sinking her, if that's what you mean.'

'If it's not unusual,' I said heavily, 'then it's about the only thing aboard this bloody ship that isn't. Though I was thinking more about her blowing *up* than sinking down – an' with us still in residence.'

John grinned deprecatingly, which did more to irritate than reassure me. 'I've salvaged more minelayers than you've had hot dinners, old boy. All full to the gun'les with mines that had been bashed, soaked, burnt . . . you name it. And I'm still here.'

I still glared at him nervously. 'Yeah? Only you didn't have Tilsley's pirates around to help, did you? And anyway, *I've* salvaged ships with holes in 'em like railway tunnels – after hitting those terribly safe mines you seem to hold in such contempt.'

He looked so patient I could've throttled him. But as I've said before, John always did have that faintly patronising air when it came to knowing things I didn't.

'Look . . . a contact mine is fired electrically, right? And the electrical energy is provided by a battery – a dry battery without any acid to make it live, right?'

'Um.'

'Now, you know the horns that stick out've the mine?'

I drew myself erect with lofty dignity. 'I am not an absolute child, Templeton.'

He didn't seem to agree. Or maybe he should have been a schoolteacher. 'Well, the horns are soft metal. And inside each one is a glass vial containing that acid – until an object strikes the horn, breaks the glass, and the acid runs into the battery to complete the firing circuit. It's quite simple really. To most people.'

I ignored the inference. 'And then . . . *Bang!*'

'No.'

It was a terrible temptation. To hit him. 'Whaddya mean . . . ?' I snarled again, '. . . *NO!*'

'Because the mine's still safe. It still needs arming – with both a detonator and a primer. And if you don't believe me, ask Tanker. He spent five years with the Mine Counter-measures crowd and he says they're safe as footballs filled with Plasticine . . . until you add the acid, the battery . . .'

'. . . the detonator and the primer.'

I turned away, reassured despite my annoyance, to gaze at *Tactician*, with Barney on her bridge, laying out the second anchor on our port quarter. 'Actually Plasticine doesn't frighten me at all. It's only things like Amatol and TNT that make me nervous . . . and obviously they wouldn't be fool enough to ship the things in the same consignment as their detonators an' stuff anyway.'

John grinned. We needed a bit of light humour to relieve

the strain and the idea of loading high explosive *and* detonators together was a bit funny in a way.

'Oh, it would be O.K. as long as they kept them apart. Stowed the dets in the strong room, say, or even . . .'

Then his grin faded and he snatched the cargo plan open for a very brief moment.

Just before he started running. Forward. To the strong room.

I shouted after him bitterly, 'They *are* on board, aren't they? Those *bloody* detonators!'

Then I began running too.

While the fear came back, even worse than before.

I finally caught up with him under the break of the fo'c'sle. We sort of jammed together in the outside door leading to the alleyway, then John gave an impatient wrench and fell through ahead of me. And stopped dead.

Someone had already been there. The strong room door still swung open to reveal a neatly stowed tier of wooden cases, each stencilled quite emphatically *Ministry of Defence* (*Navy*) HIGHLY DANGEROUS EXPLOSIVE MATERIAL.

The tier would have looked even more symmetrical without that one displaced box which lay open on top of it, tattered ears of brown greaseproof paper gaping untidily to expose the hollow in the straw packing where its contents had previously lain. Or the four hollows, to be precise. One complete, do-it-yourself mine detonating kit.

We stared at each other in sick realisation.

Until John said carefully, 'So that's it then, Peter. We call in the Algerians, and the hell with the ship!'

I bit my lip, feeling a little sick. 'Wait a minute. Let's think this thing out befo . . .'

He snapped tightly, 'We don't need to, dammit! That missing kit – the detonators – prove there's a killer . . . maybe five killers . . . loose aboard this ship. And now he, or they, have the ability to blow every last one of us to fragments.

I say we turn Tilsley, Lenz and the other three over for questioning an' risk the consequences.'

'Except we don't *risk* a damned thing, John – we get it f'r certain! Five to ten years in an Arab jail for withholding material evidence. An' that's forgetting odd charges like preventing the police in the execution of their duties. And being accessories after the fact. And maybe even . . .'

He glared at me angrily, 'So what do you suggest – that we search the whole ship for a package small enough to be hidden inside an overnight bag, huh? Or guard the mines to stop them being armed – when you know damn well it'll need ten men watching round the clock . . . and just hope the *Sarikamis* refloats herself in the meantime because our crowd'll be too busy protecting themselves to do any salvage work.'

I said slowly, 'Unless we do nothing, Johnny. Apart from take out an insurance policy.'

He grinned peevishly. 'Oh, *that's* a good idea. So we all get a million quid – just as soon as the mines blow with us still aboard.'

I shook my head. 'They won't. Not as long as Tilsley and Co. are aboard with us. And don't forget, they *are* contact mines – someone needs to hit 'em with a hammer before leaving . . . and nobody can move that fast.'

'It wouldn't be all that hard. Not to rig up some kind of delayed impact . . .'

'No. But it would be bloody dangerous, though. Look, we've seen how Tilsley and crew operate, even if they did run the *Sarikamis* aground in the first place and it wasn't her Old Man who'd flipped his lid . . .

John looked at the empty box. 'Oh, they did. That's the one thing we do know for certain now, Peter.'

'Okay! So either Tilsley or Lenz, or both. or all of them, are in it then. They're killers. But they only murder by remote control, Johnny. While they're still aboard this ship we're as safe as sitting home in front of the fire . . . because whoever drowned the *Sarikamis* sailors was damn careful not to be included in the corpses.'

He still looked doubtful. Almost as worried as I felt. But I tried to forget my fears because I still wanted very much to save our dream, and it really was all so logical and watertight as a theory.

Eventually I almost believed it myself – until I started getting more and more tired, and more and more aware that a ship is a big place. Too big to be able to keep track of any one group of men for very long.

And they wouldn't need very long. Not to slip ashore in one of the inflatables which had to be left in permanent readiness for the hundred and one tasks a salvage job requires.

After they'd inserted that missing primer, detonator and battery. And, somehow, rigged one mine to blow in the middle of all the others, just after they'd left.

Thirty-six hours later, and I was still worrying.

I think it had been the dead Second Officer's cabin. It didn't really matter, not as long as it had a bunk and a place to kick off my seaboots.

Swinging my legs up I lay back without even bothering to switch the light off, just feeling the fatigue sweeping over me in languidly seductive waves. We'd been working flat out for two solid days and nights now and this was the first break I'd allowed myself.

Yet even then I still couldn't sleep. For one thing there were too many noises from out on deck to listen to, and to try and identify. The hum of the generators feeding power to the winches and the more vibrant throb of *Tactician*'s portable 6-inch pumps as they lifted the water from number three hold; now, we hoped, patched and secure. It had only been a small gash, not much bigger than a porthole where one tooth of the Scab had penetrated – but being sixteen feet below the waterline it had still allowed six thousand tons of water to enter her every hour.

Number two hold was, miraculously, dry. John and I had hardly dared to look at each other when we sounded her to find a modest few hundred gallons per hour of seepage through buckled but still tight plates. We guessed that, when she hit the reef, she must have lifted as her forefoot took the impact, carrying her up and forward clean over number two until the inertia dropped her back down on the Scab again, dragging her to a halt before her engine space could be breached.

So somebody up there liked us – speaking strictly as a salvage man. Oh sure, the fore-peak tank was slashed open like a crushed light bulb and the bottom of the *Sarikamis* as far aft as the bridge was scarred and corrugated like an inverted tin roof. There was a gash twenty-two feet long in number one forward hold which we just had to make good before we could risk hauling her off – or trying to, anyway. But we knew we could save her if the weather held off, and the sea. And the rotten luck we'd been dogged by for six frustrating years . . .

I screwed my eyes tight and tried to force myself to sleep, but every time a roller came in under her stern the ship lurched again and a little bit of me jolted sickly with her. Then the hammering re-started as the shipwright gang turned-to after a hasty supper, fabricating the great curved patch for the rent in the forward hold to the templates already provided by Mike Tracey's diving team . . . And the gruff shouts from Tanker's rigging crew as they rove the fifty-ton blocks to the stern anchors, ready for when the time came to try and haul the *Sarikamis* back into her natural element . . .

I should have slept, but I didn't.

There were too many 'ifs' and 'buts', too many unanswered questions. There was too much guilt in my mind about what we should have reported, and didn't. And the threat which now seemed to loom even more tangibly over the eerie, isolated speck which was the *Sarikamis* because – to my exhausted mind – the most menacing thing of all was the way those five oddly-assorted men were helping us to save her, and with what even I had to admit appeared to be ungrudging conscientiousness.

Yet all the time I knew, deep down in my heart, that they intended to kill her – and us – and that the moment for dying couldn't be very far away. I even knew how they would do it, the weapon they would use, yet there wasn't a damned thing I could do to stop them. Not if I was really honest with myself.

They were going to blow us and the *Sarikamis,* and the Scab Rocks and maybe even quite a lot of Africa into flaming, spinning fragments.

They would do it with the cargo which neatly filled the upper 'tween decks of number six hold, only a few hundred feet away from where I lay.

But I wouldn't really feel it when it happened. None of us would.

Not when two hundred naval contact mines went off with a bang . . .

Funnily enough it didn't seem a terribly loud explosion, not when that first mine went off. Not half as shocking as I'd anticipated. And then there was a second slamming noise, and a third . . . and I jerked upright on the bunk to find the light still on and that it wasn't a shipload of explosives erupting after all, but that I'd finally drifted off into an uneasy, tormented half-sleep just before someone had started hammering at the cabin door.

My legs automatically hit the deck, feeling like lead-filled tubes. Then the knocking began again, even more frenziedly, and I forced myself awake and hobbled towards the door thinking, 'You're really goin' to pieces, Ross boy. Locking yourself in a cabin aboard an unstable bloody wreck . . .'

Or had I been subconsciously more frightened of the devils I didn't know . . . ? And there was another odd thing I noticed before I grabbed for the door handle – that all the noises from out on deck had stopped. That for the first time since we'd boarded the *Sarikamis* was as silent as . . .

. . . I tried not to think of a simile. All the appropriate ones had been used up a long time ago. So I opened the door instead.

I made out five words. 'Accident . . . Oh *Jesus*, Sir!' and '. . . aft!'

Then I'd started running once again, after the young kid with the chalk-white face who'd just found out that salvage and sudden horror could, on occasions, sail in company.

The after decks were bathed in the magnesium-white glare of the cargo lamps rigged high on the mainmast. Absently I noticed how black the shadows seemed against the slowly rolling vertical surfaces of the superstructure while, every few moments, there was a dull *sough* as another breaker came in under her stern and a column of spray hung bleached white against the jet black backdrop of the night.

I also realised belatedly that I hadn't even remembered to slip into my seaboots, but when I saw the way that silent group of men stood huddled under the break of the poop it didn't seem terribly important anyway.

John and Tanker were in the middle of the crush, John kneeling beside a third splayed, oddly untidy figure lying almost hidden under the barrel of a winch. When he saw me pushing roughly through the crowd John slowly rose to his feet and seemed to look helplessly round until someone thrust a hank of dirty cotton waste into his hands. Carefully he wiped them, and the blood looked very red under the glare.

'It's McKay,' he said quietly, 'Andy McKay. His skull's smashed in like a breakfast egg.'

Somebody vomited uncontrollably beside me . . . It was the young salvage hand and it made me remember the way McKay himself had retched as we walked among those grisly part-men bumping against that silver beach on the other side of the Scab.

It also made me unreasoningly angry.

I swung round violently, glaring at the grim faces confronting me. 'You heard, din't you . . . ? McKay's dead! Which means he's entitled to a bit of bloody privacy now, like not being stared at by a bunch of . . .'

John said, 'Easy, Peter.'

But he always was the one who did the right thing. Except for one instance, when he'd grudgingly agreed to go along with me, right up to our necks in the *Sarikamis* trap.

I took a grip on my frayed nerves. 'Look, we're running short of time. And there's nothing you can do. Just get back to work, boys . . . except for anyone who saw it . . . this . . . happen.'

Which was all very reasonably put. Except that nobody moved. Not one of them.

One of the riggers shuffled sullenly. It was Garrity. Not one of our most amenable crewmen at the best of times. 'None of us did. An' that's what we don't like. There's been too many queer things goin' on aboard this bloody coffin.'

I started to frown uneasily. Suddenly there was a bad feeling in the air, a menacing one. And, just for once, it didn't include the five men who'd so perceptively decided to stay instead of drown. Now it was a truculent, frightened salvage crew who stood before me. And frightened men could very easily turn into savage, dangerous men.

Stepping over, I stared at the rigger, Garrity. '. . . aboard this bloody coffin, *Sir* !'

Tanker casually moved in behind me, just like he'd done when the Brothers Mentese had threatened. I saw Garrity's eyes flicker worriedly.

'*Sir!*' he muttered. But he still didn't move.

John nudged my arm and I looked up, over the men's heads towards the centrecastle. Five figures stood watching us from the boat deck, faces impassive under the slowly swinging lights. The gross form of Lenz seemed to dominate the group, even more foreshortened by the height of his perch. White and bloated and obscene, the king spider in the *Sarikamis* web.

'You bastard!' I thought bitterly. 'It's only because of you and your mates that I'm having to handle the first stages of a near mutiny. Only the irony of it is that you're the crowd who'll get it in the neck if the boys here do run amok. And personally I don't give a damn one way or the other – except that another few deaths'll have every Bedouin bobby from the Sahara north clambering over this boat and asking why . . .'

I said grimly, 'Okay! Who found him?'

There was a stir amongst the group, then the young salvage hand who'd called me pushed hesitantly forward, still looking as though he'd liked to have spent a bit longer being sick. 'Me, Sir. The Bosun sent me aft to check on the stern anchor lines. I got half way up the poop ladder an' glanced back . . . There was a foot under the winch an' . . . an' then I found Andy. And the blood . . .'

'Anyone else around?'

'Jus' me. And Andy McKay . . .'

Garrity snarled, 'It must've been them. Those bastards who stayed aboard. That poncy mate an' the fat Kraut an' that . . . so let's make bloody certain they don't do nothing else before . . .'

'Belay that!'

John's voice was like a guillotine. He moved forward beside the winch barrel and gestured. 'If anyone smashed McKay's skull in, then they lifted a two-ton winch to do it with . . You, Garrity! Come here!'

He grabbed the rigger's arm and literally dragged the man over to the winch. 'Look, damn it! Blood, brains, hair . . . smeared right across the flange. He fell, Garrity. Off the bloody ladder like a first-trip apprentice . . . which means it was an accident. McKay killed *himself*!'

I thought tightly, 'Thank God they don't know about the missing detonators . . .' as Garrity shuffled uncomfortably, staring uneasily at the glistening mess on the winch barrel. Someone else muttered in a low voice, 'Mind you, he always was a clumsy bastard, was Andy,' and the crowd seemed to relax a little.

I glanced up at the centrecastle. The five watchers still hadn't moved, yet oddly enough I got that same impression I'd had earlier – that even the opposition weren't entirely in accord with each other. That there were two factions with separate interests watching us. Tilsley and possibly the highly-strung Third Officer Burak on the one hand, with fat, menacing Lenz on the other side of a nebulous fence in company with the sinister Brothers Mentese, our Turkish Twins with an affinity for knives and hooded glances.

Another breaker came in under the stern, almost below us. But this time it didn't just sigh as it broke, it slammed apart with a muffled roar and the deck jumped three or four feet vertically. A curtain of spray twinkled briefly against the lamps before it spattered across the tense faces before me and I thought bitterly, 'That's it, then. That's all we bloody need. Now even the lousy weather's starting to break up . . .'

Everyone felt it. The eyes of Tactician's seamen glanced uneasily outboard, out to where the riding lights of the tug carved spirals against the darkness. She was rolling too, I could tell immediately, recoiling from the first indications of the bigger seas building to the north west. And after the seas would come the wind, punching the faces of the waves into near-vertical walls of power which would move relentlessly against the stranded Sarikamis, lifting her bodily and throwing her forward against the Scab like a flotsam light bulb . . .

So we had even less time than we'd hoped for. Only nobody was doing anything about it. Men I would have trusted to follow me anywhere a week ago were now – under the influence of that almost tangible aura of death which hung over the *Sarikamis* – defying me with a virtually mutinous hostility.

Until Tanker stepped forward. And Tanker was a superlative psychologist. He understood men like Garrity, and knew just how to coax the best out of them. So he chummily put his craggy features very close to the equally hard rigger's countenance.

And said, quite sincerely, 'Jus' get back to work, Garrity . . . or I'll smash your fucking face in!'

This time, grudgingly, they went. But I knew it was only a temporary reprieve, and it didn't make me feel one little bit better. Just more confused and apprehensive.

Grimly the three of us stood, watching them shuffle forward in an unsettling, close-knit body, until they disappeared along the starboard alleyway. There were actually four of us left on that spray-dappled afterdeck, but the last in our company wasn't very interested in what the *Sarikamis* promised any more because he didn't have anything left to be frightened of.

John said quietly, 'Maybe it wasn't an accident, Peter.'

I nodded absently, thinking about the detonators again. 'No? Well, I didn't really imagi . . .'

Then the full import of what he'd said hit me. I swung round in shock as Tanker shrugged at me across McKay's sprawled corpse. 'It was murder, Skipper. Garrity was right . . . except I wasn't goin' to tell that bolshie bastard nothing.'

'How?' Even as I spoke I was automatically glancing up towards the only men who could have been responsible but they'd gone too. The boat deck rail was empty. Which was O.K. by me.

John looked pointedly down towards what had been McKay's head and I felt a bit silly. I added tightly, 'I mean – if he didn't fall, then he must've been hit with something. And you said yourself, a two-ton winch is a helluva hammer.'

'We don't know yet. But we think he was killed up on

the poop deck, then hauled down here and set up to make it look natural. Even down to the details like blood and brai . . .'

I snapped quickly, 'Yeah, yeah! But how do you know all that?'

Tanker jerked his thumb. 'There's more of it up there. Not very much 'cause whoever did it swilled the deck over, only the water didn't dry off quick enough before the kid found McKay.'

'And does *he* know?'

'Not him. One glance an' he took off yellin' like a banshee. Only reason I saw the evidence was because I had a pretty good idea why McKay *was* killed. Only I had to go right up on the poop deck to check it out.'

The deck moved sullenly again, lifting to the seas then snubbing hard as the starboard-quarter anchor took the strain, preventing her from broaching-to parallel with, and against, the Scab.

And suddenly I knew why McKay had died too.

I scrambled up the ladder to the high poop deck. The wind caught me as I rose above the shelter of the well deck, snapping the collar of my reefer irritably, and I thought, 'Hell! Three or four hours more and this could build up to gale force . . .' Then I saw precisely what I'd anticipated and I stopped dead with the shock of it, because even when you do expect something bad you still feel the real horror when it actually happens.

John came up behind me and I looked at him miserably. He shrugged. 'That proves it beyond any doubt, Peter. Someone really *is* trying to make sure the *Sarikamis* never comes off this reef.'

I walked to the rail and looked over. A streamer of spray whipped across the poop, spattering along the deck with a long drawn hiss, but I ignored it, searching through the blackness for the wire leading to the starboard anchor. Every so often a whitecapped wave reared luminously to dissolve immediately in a fading smother of foam, and it was against one of those lighter patches that I finally made out the wire rising from the sea.

Even as I watched it pulled tight as the ship rolled away, then the softly gleaming strand sagged again towards the surface while the roller moved in below me. My eyes followed the wire upwards until it was led inboard through the fairlead, bulkily disguised by the burlap cushioning we'd fitted to prevent chafe. Still bar tight the wire then ran forward to the figure of eight turns around the bitts – those twin-steel bollards that you invariably fall over instead of walk around on a dark night – then forward again through the second set of bitts until, finally, the end of the wire secured around the barrel of the starboard poop winch.

Except that, in this particular case, the wire ended in an untidy mess of coils where someone had recently cast off both the winch and forward bitts fastenings. The *Sarikamis* was now only secured by a half-dozen turns of wire which could be let go in less than sixty seconds.

It meant that, if McKay had lived for that one minute longer before he surprised whoever had been so industriously sabotaging our lifeline, then all I might have felt by now would have been the screeching vibration of tearing plates as we broadsided irretrievably against the Scab . . .

If we were right. And our over-active imaginations weren't making too much out of a carried-away wire rope, and a still-wet patch of seawater where the spray encroached anyway.

But I said savagely, 'From now on we keep a watch up here. Maybe there's nothing we can do about those missing detonators, but by God we can make damn sure this doesn't happen again. Not without a fight.'

Tanker picked up a length of piping lying in the scuppers. He hefted it experimentally and I couldn't help wondering if it had already killed one man that night, but it looked clean and the chances were that any murder weapon was already overboard and purified by the sea. And we were a bit short of forensic investigators in our salvage crew.

He hefted it again, looking very satisfied. 'I hope someone does try it on a second time. In fact I'd like that a lot.'

I said tiredly, 'O.K. If you stay here for now we'll send someone to see about McKay . . .'

It was only when John and I were back amidships that John said irritably, 'I thought you said we *shouldn't* tell anyone about the stolen detonators?'

I shrugged. 'Well I haven't. So what?'

He stopped and looked at me a bit strangely, 'But I haven't either, Peter.'

'I never suggested you had. And seeing we agreed not to, I don't . . .'

And then I ground to a halt as well, staring back at him as the inference slowly registered.

'*Tanker* . . . ?'

He shrugged, but I could detect the sudden concern in his eyes.

'It's just the ship,' he said uncertainly. 'There's a sort of atmosphere about her . . . a bloke starts imagining things, Peter. Don't you sense it too?'

'Oh, I sense it,' I muttered, dropping my gaze. 'Too damn right I sense it.'

But I still didn't want to look straight at him. You see, I couldn't help thinking that, this time, it wasn't just the ship. Or our imagination.

Because when I'd thoughtlessly mentioned the missing detonators our trusted Bosun hadn't batted an eyelid. Had never looked surprised or curious or anything . . .

Which could only mean that Tanker had *already* known about the theft from the strong room.

And Tanker was also the one certain man aboard the *Sarikamis* who would know precisely how to arm a naval contact mine.

And how to detonate it by remote control.

Perhaps, unconsciously, that niggling little uncertainty about Tanker was the last straw. But either way, while we both pretended that McKay's death was the only reason, we also knew now we would have to compromise. To involve the authorities even if it meant forfeiting any last hopes of ever saving the *Sarikamis*.

I'd glanced at my watch under the glare of the lamps. It was 3.20 in the morning. John said flatly, 'Call Algiers now, Peter. On the radio.'

I shook my head doggedly. 'There's still a chance. We'll bring *Tactician* alongside at first light and pack Tilsley and company off to Djidjelli. It'll take the locals a fair time to sort out what's what and, while they do, we might just get this bloody boat in the water . . . *without* having to keep looking over our shoulders in case some odd sod's creeping up with a club.'

He frowned hesitantly. 'And Tanker? What about him, Peter?'

'Forget it. Probably we're wrong. Or maybe he's got his own perfectly good reasons for keeping quiet. Just let's get rid of our Turkish puzzles an' work like hell.'

John smiled at me for the first time in days. I think we both felt a lot better right then, now that the decision had been taken. 'I'll go and break the news to Tilsley and Lenz,' he grinned. 'Give them plenty of time to get their toothbrushes and alibis ready.' I smiled back until, two minutes later, all my good humour had vanished.

First there was a clatter of feet on the ladder above me and Eddie Styles came sliding down, waving a paper. When he saw me he skidded to a halt and looked terribly rugged and capable. 'Weather report, Skipper. We'd better prepare for strong to gale force winds in the next few hou . . .'

His voice trailed off as I gently took the forecast out of his hand and tore it into little pieces. The force six wind which had been increasing for the last half hour scattered the fragments in seconds.

I said wearily, 'Call the tug. Tell Barney to prepare the line thrower in case our stern anchors drag, and to be alongside at 0800 anyway. To pick up passengers.'

Then the prospective passengers arrived, looking somewhat aggressively truculent, and Eddie had vanished with all the expertise of a dedicated coward.

Tilsley shouted, 'You've no damn right to order us ashore, Ross. You're just the hired help, remember?'

I swung round with the blood surging uncontrollably to my head. He still looked as debonair as ever, the curiously out of place Englishman, but very, very upset. Just like a Chief Officer would look, if he'd been told to leave his own ship.

But I snarled back regardlessly, 'And you're too expensive a luxury, Tilsley. One, or maybe even all of you, have cost a whole human life already. Back there on the poop!'

He looked at me narrowly. 'You told your men it was an accident. We all heard you.'

'Yeah. Well if it was, McKay smashed his own head in before he dragged his body thirty feet down a ladder, smeared blood an' brains over a winch barrel, then lay down under it to die . . . *after* virtually letting go the starboard anchor wire!'

There was a sharp intake of breath and I saw Burak, the Turkish Third Mate, take a step backward in horror. But it was the reaction of the man standing beside him that intrigued me the most – that of Lenz the mammoth Teuton.

'You make a terrible accusation, *Kapitan*,' he said, looking so genuinely shocked that even I wondered a little about his real feelings. 'And why *should* any of us wish to do such a criminal thing, hah?'

And I almost believed he really meant it. Except I had the vague impression that the gross Lenz wasn't concerned quite

98

so much with the identity of the man who'd split McKay's skull with a crowbar, as with the fact that whoever it was had been bloody minded enough to try to untie the boat as well.

But that was the most unsettling factor in the whole crazy *Sarikamis* horror story – because while logic told me those five men *had* to be the ones who wanted her destroyed, their reactions and recent conduct had suggested a precisely opposite resolve . . . to save the ship with every bit of assistance they could offer.

Especially Lenz. My prime suspect for the role of King Villain had been working like a beaver alongside Tanker in organising and encouraging . . . I stopped. I had a brief vision of Lenz and Tanker together earlier, heads close and engaged in deep conversation about some technical point – or had it been a problem involving salvage? Though why else would Lenz wish to discuss anything with Tanker . . . ?

Tanker.

Again.

And the unreasoning apprehension clamped down over my judgement like a shroud. I snapped, 'I don't know why you should or shouldn't want to, Lenz. But I don't know why this ship ran aground in the first place either, and what's more, I don't give a damn one way or the other. I'm just going to let you explain that to the local boys while I get on with salvaging her.'

Tilsley said, 'I told you, Ross. Captain Koroglu ran her into Ras oum Achiche . . . *and* all the rest of it.'

I nodded. 'Oh, I believe you, Mister. And of course you and all the other officers sat down below over a nice cup of tea while the Old Man went quietly mad, huh?'

'It happened during the morning watch, the eight to twelve, Ross. That *is* the Captain's watch in case you didn't know. I handed over to Koroglu before breakfast and spent the time before we hit this reef working in my office. I don't keep looking out to see if the Captain's steering the ship on the right track.'

I shrugged. 'But you must have had some idea, even with the fog. Any seaman would know approximately what course they were on . . . the wind, the set of the sea? Come off it, Tilsley – even you should have sensed you were heading into this bay instead of west, towards Gib.'

He grinned nastily. 'But I did, Mister . . . because we were *supposed* to be heading this way. Or didn't you think to check on where we were making for?'

'Where?' Somehow I had the uneasy feeling I was not only losing this argument, but that I was also presenting a badly prepared case.

'Djidjelli, our next loading port . . . Seven hundred tons of cork, Ross. The local product. Which means that Koroglu only had to bring her a few degrees east to hit the cliffs. A virtually undetectable alteration to anyone other than the watchkeeping navigator – in this case the Old Man himself.'

The wind whipped in under the deckhead and Tilsley's hair ruffled unheeded. I half noticed there was a lot more white foam out there against the blackness of the sea but I was more concerned with the look of apparent sincerity in the *Sarikamis* Chief Officer's eyes. And if he was sincere, and Lenz was also just a bloody good, loyal-to-his-owners sailorman, then . . .

Burak!

'What about him – your Third Mate? I snapped. 'He would have been on the eight to twelve too, along with Koroglu?'

The young kid jumped as though I'd struck him across the face. 'I am sent off the bridge, Sir. The Captain, he say to me "Go and check up on the lifeboat stores. I will navigate the sheep . . ." '

He stared anxiously at me, almost as if willing me to believe him. I shook my head dazedly, trying to grasp that one remote factor which still eluded me. That one flaw in the otherwise almost believable story of how a ship committed suicide. Hell, even the Third Mate's being sent to check out the boats would add up, if Koroglu intended to sink her . . .

'The helmsman? You were heading for those cliffs a long

time after they must have been in visual contact . . . and nobody steers straight into a brick wall, no matter who orders it!'

Tilsley spread his hands in a gesture which suggested he'd not stayed entirely British during his spell in the Turkish Merchant Navy. 'We were running on auto-pilot, Ross. This is a modern ship . . . not like some I've seen recently.'

And I knew precisely what he meant. Even his eyes were turned outwards, towards where *Tactician*'s lights spiralled crazily now as she slammed into the rising weather. I glanced over to where Lenz, flanked as ever by the two Menteses, seemed to be watching and . . . my mind took another strange turn of fancy . . . and almost assessing. Almost judging, like I was, whether Tilsley and Burak were really telling the truth.

As if the fat man, too, was trying to learn the real reason why the *Sarikamis* had come to grief.

And *that* was the craziest assumption of all!

Except I knew, beyond any doubt, that it was precisley what the German Bosun was doing. Tilsley was on trial before people other than myself.

I jerked my heads upwards, towards the bridge. 'There was a fight, a scuffle, just after you turned away from the cliffs and before you tried to run us down. Who got nasty with who, Tilsley?'

'I came up on the bridge and saw what was happening. Koroglu was out on the wing . . . I hit the full right-rudder button on the auto-pilot, rang the starboard engine to astern, then tried to tackle him . . .' He hesitated, '. . . He was like a crazy man, Ross. Screaming and raving at me, then he hit me and, when I knew what was happening again, the ship was aground and the Old Man bawling "Abandon ship" like it was the only way to stay alive . . .'

'But it wasn't, was it? So why did they all go? Except for you five?'

'Because they panicked. And when the Captain says "Go", Ross, then by God you *go* . . .'

I raised an eyebrow nastily. 'I say again, Tilsley – *you* didn't. You all stuck together like glue while your mates drowned.'

'*Nein!*'

The vehemence of Lenz's denial surprised even me. I swung to face him warily. 'Nein, *Kapitan* Ross! I was in the paint store with the two men ⋅ Mentese here when she struck this reef. The door was jammed by the force of the grounding. And when we came out we found them all gone . . . except for *this*.'

He gestured towards Tilsley contemptuously, but the Mate just stared back at his junior rating with anything but the affronted dignity one would normally anticipate under such circumstances. It proved, beyond any doubt in my mind, that the gulf between Lenz and Tilsley was greater than any conspiracy to sink the *Sarikamis* could justify.

And that, in its turn, suggested that at least one of them was telling the truth. But who?

I said sharply, 'You still haven't answered, Tilsley . . . Why did you stay aboard, when it was your duty to go in the boats?'

He didn't say anything for a further moment. He was still staring white-faced at the man Lenz. And then he turned slowly towards me and looked very lost indeed.

'I couldn't stop them abandoning, Ross, there was too much panic for that. Only Burak would listen to me. But I knew I was a dead man too, if I went in those boats . . .'

He took a deep breath and, once again, I felt that grudging sympathy for the man who seemed like me in so many ways, and who could just possibly be a victim of circumstance.

Then he said, very quietly, 'Would you really have gone yourself, Ross . . . knowing you would have been dead in another two or three minutes?'

And when I'd thought about the answer – honestly thought about it – I knew I had to let them stay aboard the *Sarikamis* until I could be sure.

By then I was even having doubts about whether we'd ever

heard an impossible Mayday call, made a long time before a ship even reached its wrecking place. And *had* McKay really been murdered . . . ? Or could he have died by accident after all? Maybe half way through the act of letting the anchor cable go – striking back at the ship out of some twisted conviction that she was responsible for the mutilation of his friend, that time she tried to run us down.

Only none of those wild theories explained the theft of one contact mine detonating kit.

But someone else could have done that. And I trusted him too implicitly to doubt his motives.

Well, I *did*, dammit!

Didn't I . . . ?

Oh, I had a hell of a row with John when I told him. We stood out there while the wind gusted even more violently, snatching at our clothes with greedy, probing fingers. And the seas piled up in excited mounds of foam, clutching at the stern of the wreck as though impatient to taste their coming victory.

And the cargo clusters swinging in ever increasing para-bolas, great rings of yellow light skating and gyrating crazily across the heaving, shuddering deck while, over all, the hammering and the shouts of the salvage crew were some-times overwhelmed by the screaming of tortured metal as the *Sarikamis*'s already flooded bows ground deeper and deeper into the clutches of the Scab.

But John had to agree eventually. It wasn't even a question of choice, really. For one thing we both knew it would be too rough to bring *Tactician* alongside at this stage, to take off Tilsley and Lenz and the others. And the same conditions would prevent any police craft from bringing either reinforcements or investigators.

Though even if they did come, they still wouldn't do a damned thing. Because they would believe Tilsley's story of Koroglu's last crazed hours – only we would still have lost the

Sarikamis for ever because the only thing we'd really proved was that we were unfit to be trusted any longer. We'd still withheld evidence . . .

. . . so we locked McKay's poor, distorted corpse in an empty cabin, and worked like hell. And waited.

For either the weather, or the five enigmatic men among us, or two hundred Amatol-packed sea mines . . . to try and kill us. Again!

CHAPTER NINE

Needless to say everything seemed to go so well for the next sixteen hours that, occasionally, I had to pinch myself to prove I was still awake.

The huge patch was virtually completed, ready for securing over the great rent in number one forward hold. The weather, while still promising worse to come, had temporarily steadied at around force five to six . . . which was like a summer zephyr to a salvage man. Mike Tracey's divers reported that the ship was still snugly embedded into the anchor point of the Scab forward, while, leading from astern, those two critical holding wires showed no signs of dragging. They showed no signs of being tampered with any further either, but maybe that was because John and Tanker between them had virtually mounted a constant watch over the poop. Mostly John, certainly, because he had a lot of calculations to do anyway. And perhaps neither of us had quite the same faith in Tanker since our niggling, almost ashamed doubts, about the strong room theft.

Even our five pervertedly incomprehensible resident threats had worked with the fury of desperate men. Tilsley and Burak on soundings and measurements while Lenz and his Turkish Duo tossed baulks of timber around like matchsticks, an exhibition which demolished, once and for all, any impressions I may have formed about the pudding-styled German's physical inadequacy.

Hell, I even smiled at him once. Until I realised it was Lenz I was staring absently towards, then I changed the grin to a truculent you-watch-it-'cause-I'm-watching-you expression

He still smiled promisingly back, though – like an S.S.

Guard, as seen from the inmate's side of the electrified fence.

It suggested it was all too good to last. And it didn't.

At ten minutes past eight that night a rather chastened Chief Radio Operator Styles handed me yet another weather forecast. He didn't look rugged this time, or hard. Just tired, and maybe a bit apprehensive about what I'd do to this particular offering.

It said uncompromisingly . . . WINDS GALE TO STRONG GALE FORCE 8 TO 9 IMMEDIATE . . .

I folded the message form, smoothed a neat crease down the middle of it, and handed it back to him very, very gently. He looked surprised at the way I'd so mildly accepted this particular notice of impending disaster, but salvage skippers are notoriously unstable when it comes to seeing a week's work being washed off a rock like a stick of marooned firewood

'Call *Tactician* again, Eddie. Stand by our stern, line thrower ready and towing wires . . . and mattresses aft in case we have to leave in a hurry.'

He muttered, 'Aye, aye, Skipper,' looking terribly grim, and wandered back up to the *Sarikamis*'s radio room holding the forecast between two fingers like a piece of white-hot tin plate.

By quarter past I'd collected Tanker, John and Mike Tracey together, Mike still wearing his wetsuit and looking as if he slept in the thing – or maybe he really did have black rubber skin with 'Dunlop' stamped all over it.

I said, 'How's the patch for number one, Tanker?'

He shrugged. 'We only need to weight it for negative buoyancy an' she's ready. Give me an hour?'

'Mike . . . ? Would your boys be prepared to dive in the dark? Say, starting at 2130.'

Tracey looked at me. 'It's dodgy, Skipper. I mean they work in the dark mostly anyway – below surface. But they've already spent well over the norm in diving time since the job started. And there's always the chance of an accident. Finding a bloke floating on the surface isn't easy in this weather, even in broad daylight.'

John chewed his lip. I could see the lines of fatigue tracing little creases round the corners of his eyes. 'Can't we leave it until morning, Peter? With sinkers that patch weighs far in excess of the safe working load of the derricks. I'd like to test the gear before we go ahead.'

I knew what he meant, what they both meant.

Apart from the obvious risk to the salvage crew if several tons of heavy lift carried away there was also the end product of days of highly specialised effort in hazard. And one which neither the deteriorating weather nor the already bar-taut strain on the men's nerves and morale would allow us to repeat.

Fabricating that patch, and the final application of it over the gash in the *Sarikamis*'s hull, was our solitary ace in the pack. And we could only play it once – a win all, lose all gamble which, under any other circumstances, would only be taken when the conditions were absolutely right.

Our hand had been in preparation since that first morning aboard the wreck. Firstly Mike's diving team had surveyed the damage, reporting that the rent not only ran for twenty-two feet fore and aft, but also gaped under the starboard bilge as far as the tank margin plate. It meant that not only did we have to fashion a patch snug enough to follow the turn of that bilge, but that we would also have to allow a second curvature identical with the form of the ship as it narrowed towards the bow.

And that, to withstand the tons of water pressure which would be applied as soon as the *Sarikamis* eased off the Scab, the whole deliberately distorted patch would require to be fabricated in baulks of timber of at least six by twelve inches in section.

Which was a helluva carpentry problem, even when your woodworking bench isn't jumping up and down like a yo-yo and you're so tired you have to make a conscious effort to stop your hand following the length of timber you're splitting into the blur of the circular saw blade.

So the task had started. The divers first again, working largely by touch in the surging undertow to fashion rough templates which would both follow the curvature and also allow the edges of the final patch to bed on sound plating. Then, while they carried on with cutting away the razor-sharp, distorted edges of the gaping tear, we used the canvas of number three hatch as a moulding loft floor and ever so carefully drew out, full scale, the final design of the patch itself.

Eventually John and I, and Tanker and the shipwrights, all decided that the whole bloody job was impossible . . . and then we went right ahead and did it anyway.

But that was the salvage trade.

And when we'd finished we caulked every seam before fitting an oakum and burlap pad on the inside of the huge plug so that it would be snug as an Eskimo's blanket against the *Sarikamis*'s bottom . . .

Just before Eddie Styles handed me a weather forecast which more or less suggested that we should throw the whole bloody lot overboard and take up farming for a living.

Because we still had to hoist that mammoth, unmanageable nightmare out over the side of the ship – excess-weighted so it would sink below the surface – and then attach the wires already prepared and running over the port bulwarks, under the bottom of the *Sarikamis*, and up over the starboard side, to the lower edge of the suspended patch in order to draw it in to the ship's hull once it was lowered into position.

And all that on undersized cargo-handling gear, with bar-taut wires thrumming through over-heating blocks suspended on utterly inadequate derricks . . . and all the time with the ship rolling and pitching as the ever increasing seas shook her like a rag doll, and poor lighting to lure an already half-asleep man into a corner where a snapping wire would slice him clean in half before he could even scream . . . and divers waiting in the pitch black water right under the juggernaut they had to guide into place . . .

Mind you, after *that* it was easy. All we had to do then was to start pumping out the flooded number one hold and just hope to God the Heath Robinson contraption fitted in the first place, and that the whole lot wouldn't cave in like a bubble in a vacuum as the outside pressure overcame the hold pressure, clamping the patch against the open wound like a giant hydraulic press.

And then we just emptied the hold, caulked and cemented the thing from the inside, pulled eight thousand tons of boat off a reef which gripped her as if wrecks were going out of fashion, towed or steamed her a few hundred miles through what promised to be a force ten storm . . . if nobody in particular didn't just happen to open her seacocks by accident while we were doing it, or start a mutiny, or set her on fire. Or perhaps just screw a shiny little detonator into any one of two hundred Amatol-packed mines . . .

I said flatly, 'There's a wind coming. It's now or never, boys.'

And, just for a brief moment, rather hoped someone would have the guts to say – 'Never!'

Only nobody did. But *that* was the salvage trade too.

We were finally ready for the big lift just before midnight.

It seemed unnaturally quiet, up there on the foredeck of the stranded *Sarikamis*. Even the white, floodlit bulk of the centre-castle helped to break the blustery attack of the gale while the movement underfoot was much less violent, this forward section being restrained by the very enemy we were fighting – the reef itself.

But it was only a fleeting impression of calm. Put your head over the bulwarks, into the wind itself, and you could feel the battering force of it, making your eyes smart with involuntary tears while your hair plastered flat down over your flayed skin in a buffeting, fluttering fringe.

And then you'd glance down to avoid the assault of it, and all you'd see would be the black oil of the incoming swell, now building up to a height where it was already becoming unstable, so that the crests of the waves couldn't keep their balance any longer and started to collapse into themselves, long streaks of white foam tracing spider's webs down the lee faces of the sea.

You might even turn your head away from the gale, towards the bows and the invisible shore. But you wouldn't like that any better, because then all you'd see – only a cable's length forward of you – would be a boiling, roaring welter of spume stretching horizontally, away from the bows, until it, too, was lost in the surrounding darkness. And they would be the claws of the Scab you were staring at in such horrified fascination, so you would decide not to look any more in case your nerve broke completely and you'd push yourself away from the rail . . . except that, just for a frightening moment, you found yourself still pinned against it. Because all the time the ship was rolling steadily, urging you to move automatically and unaware . . . until you tried to overcome the forces of equilibrium, and the ship gently reminded you that you couldn't . . .

Like it would remind us when we tried to guide a six-ton deadweight patch outboard and into position, using critically loaded untested derricks and gear. Only the reminder wouldn't be so gentle when we attempted to force that particular juggernaut to swing the other way. The way the ship didn't want it to go . . .

John called calmly, 'Take the strain. Easy now . . .'

I watched critically, feeling the nervous tension draining away as it always did once an operation had started. We were committed now, one way or the other, and professional concentration had taken the place of apprehension. For the moment.

The starboard lifting winches hummed as the power came on. Ever so slowly the barrels began to rotate, the oiled wires leading on to them like a sleekly glistening serpent. The fall of the wires, leading from the standing – or lifting – derricks, tightened in sympathy and I heard the squeak of steel against steel as the eyeplates in the top of the patch took the strain. Then the hum of the winches dropped to a low growl as the huge framework started to move.

There was a movement beside me and I sensed, rather than saw, someone standing there. A match flared and Tilsley said casually, 'You really think that tackle can stand the strain, Ross?'

I glanced at him irritably, then noticed Burak as well, staring almost hypnotically at the slowly rising slab of twisted timber. It struck me then that the *Sarikamis*'s young Third Mate always managed to stand out from his fellow crewmen. That while the other four appeared reasonably normal, balanced people despite our suspicions, Burak invariably gave the impression of living on the edge of a nightmare – that something hideous was eating his mind away and that, maybe very soon now, he would . . . snap?

But why? And was it merely a symptom of a naturally unstable mind under abnormal circumstances? Or was there something else. Something which Burak still anticipated. Or dreaded?

Something involving the *Sarikamis*. And the men aboard her . . .

I ignored Tilsley, angry with myself for allowing my attention to wander during the most critical part of the salvage programme. The patch was almost clear of the deck now, still rising smoothly, and John called a warning, 'Easy . . . easyyyyy . . . Hold her there.'

And the whole framework stopped, swinging fractionally as the riggers controlling the preventer wires took in the slack. I half bent at the knees to get a line of sight through to the rail of the bulwarks over which it had to pass. John had judged it perfectly, six clear inches as the rig was persuaded outboard.

And into the full force of that chuckling, ambushing gale.

Someone stepped forward, almost under the lift, and a torch flicked on, playing over the eyeplates with a probing yellow stare. It was Lenz, still looking hugely cumbersome but also undeniably competent as, unexpectedly, he examined the shackles for the last time before the next stage of the operation commenced. With a faint sense of surprise I found that, for the very first time, I was watching the fat man with the appreciation of a fellow seafarer, and not as a hostile critic.

Behind, and above me, Tanker's voice called calmly from the fo'c'sle winch controlling the yardarm derrick – the critical force which would jolly the whole framework outboard and into position for lowering. 'Ready when you are . . . but mind an' keep her hove tight until she's clear of the side, top men!'

Garrity, my stroppy rigger operating one of the lifting winches, glowered back at the Bosun. It was that same truculent stare he'd given me over McKay's body the previous night. 'You handle your end, Bosun. I look after mine my way . . .'

John snapped irritably. 'Oh shut up, Garrity! Heave away easily!'

The winches started to turn again and, high above us, the derrick-head blocks squealed in protest as the strain came on them. I glanced up anxiously as the topping lifts began to thrum under tension while the gently swinging rig broad-sided hugely across the deck. Beside me Tilsley and Burak seemed to be poised, almost waiting for the first screech of trouble – but then again, anyone who isn't frightened of a parted wire flailing amok on a restricted deck is either very brave or very, very stupid.

Ten feet to the bulwarks. Eight . . . seven . . . The first fingers of the gale curled around the centrecastle and stroked the curved face of the patch with hungry feelers. The faces of the winchmen turned together, following the track of the lift like a slow motion replay of a Wimbledon audience. I noticed Tanker's expression, clear and with only the faintest suspicion of the intense concentration he was applying to the task, playing the winch controls with the delicate touch of the true virtuoso. Garrity too, confident and almost casual, eyes unblinkingly watching the rig as his jaws clamped methodically in gum-chewing detachment.

Four feet . . . three . . . The ship lifted sullenly and, above the howl of the wind carried a deeper, more powerful thunder as the roller passed under us to atomise against the Scab. I saw John's eyes glance outboard for a moment, worriedly. 'Keep her going, boys . . . steady . . .'

Over the bulwarks now, carved against the blackness by the reflection of the cargo lamps. Swinging harder, starting to revolve as the gale took the edge of it until the steadying preventer lines took the train. A badly laid turn flaked off a bollard and Lenz's guttural snarl '*Dummkopf!*'

'An' eff you too, Fatso!' Pure Anglo-Saxon. I grinned tightly despite myself.

Clear of the side now but starting to oscillate more violently . . . Divers already in the water, upturned masks twinkling against the heaving nothingness, continually overwhelmed by the tumbling crests as they waited in impossible conditions . . . The whole ship leaning over to starboard with the derricks beginning to bounce rhythmically. Easy, Johnny . . . Don't let her go too far . . .

And then I felt it. Some sixth sense making me glance aft, towards the invisible horizon and the gyrating stars of *Tactician*'s distant steaming lights. And the Wave.

At first I couldn't even see it, yet somehow I knew it was out there. A rogue sea, larger than the rest. Sweeping in towards us almost as if the frustrated gale had secretly called on its second-line reserve. Rearing and foaming and tumbling . . . I started running towards John, the fear of what could happen already a dry lump in my throat.

'Avast heaving! Brakes on the winches . . . Take up the

slack on the preventers an' make fast!'

John whirled. 'F'r *Chris* . . . !'

'*Tsunami*, Johnny! We've no choice . . . Screw everything up tight, belay the preventers an' get the hell out've it!'

He stared over my shoulder and I turned, following his eyes. And saw it for the first time. And we *could* see it now. Even through the blackness.

Maybe it wasn't a *Tsunami* – a proper inshore wave like the kind we'd seen around the Japanese coasts – but by God it was big enough to freeze the blood in a man's veins for as long as it takes to drown him. Ten, fifteen feet high, with the foaming crest of it painting an eerie bluish phosphorescent line for a mile on either side of us as it constantly spilled over and down the rearing face of the monster, close enough now for us to hear the dull roar of its advance . . .

Some of the men were already running aft, making for the security of the higher centrecastle decks. I noticed, with an oddly warm surge of pride, that they'd done everything they could to minimise any movement of the still suspended patch before they went – and it was that which could cost us the *Sarikamis* because movement, under stress, takes charge and as the swing overcomes the inertia of a heavy object it begins to rampage with ever increasing violence, snapping at the restraints which hold it . . .

Maybe quarter of a mile away now. Advancing at . . . say twenty knots. We had less than fifty seconds before it struck.

There were only a few of us left on the well deck now, with the approaching roar loud enough almost to drown the last shouts of command issued by John. 'Everyone aft! Garrity . . . get the hell out've it, man! And you, Lenz. Take your boys *off* the well deck . . . !'

I stared, feeling more confused than ever. Lenz and the two Menteses were still working with the preventer stays, backing the wires to other bollards further aft for greater security . . . and if anything could ever prove that those particular survivors from the *Sarikamis* crew were here by chance and not by choice, then . . .

'The divers!' John was leaning out over the rail, staring urgently down towards the already surging water. I shouted, 'Leave them, Johnny. They'll go deep and hang on. More chance that way.'

'Garrity!'

Tanker had finished screwing down the winch and was sliding deckwards, using only his hands as runners on the polished rails of the fo'c'slehead ladder. 'Get out've that bloody seat, Garrity, an' do what you're told!'

I whirled. The recalcitrant rigger was still fumbling desperately with his winch controls. The casual expression was gone now and I caught the glint of sweat against the arc lamps. He seemed to be having trouble with the brake and even as I watched he slammed the barrel in reverse and gently applied power to hold the abandoned deadweight of the patch steady.

His voice lashed back in a bloody-minded half-scream. 'Fuck you, Bosun . . . ! The brake won't hold an' I'm doin' my job my bloody way, so jus' . . .'

And then I felt, rather than saw, the Sarikamis's after end starting to rise like an express lift and I grabbed John, hauling him bodily towards the ladder. He yelled, 'Garrity! We've got to get Garrity, Peter!' But I bawled back, 'No time, Johnny. She's already going . . .'

The deck heaved below my feet, travelling forward bodily as the Tsunami gripped her. From below I heard the horrifying shriek as the Scab welcomed the added pressure of her surge, then the thunder drowned everything but that little voice in my head which kept crying, 'This is it, Ross. That bloody old Dragon's never forgiven you for the two fingers at the Vespasian . . .'

Somebody big and solid slammed into us, growled 'Shit!' and grabbed for a handhold. It was Tanker. He added succinctly, 'Garrity! I couldn't get to him. Stupid, stubborn bastard!'

Then the sea came inboard and it was the *Vespasian* all over again, with that gurgling, tearing pressure plucking at our bodies and the whole bloody world a surging, liquid bedlam. I clawed myself erect, searching desperately for the patch until I saw it, still stark against the blackness but swinging now, tearing at the bonds which restrained it. Tons of deadweight moving more and more savagely as the ship reared and grated against the reef.

There was a *crack*! A gunshot in the night. And Garrity's winch started to clatter abruptly as the tension on the barrel suddenly eased.

I saw him then, riding the bucking steel seat like some outrageous opera cowboy in the saddle. But there wasn't anything of the old aggressive Garrity in the sweat-shiny face now. Only the wild-eyed look of a frightened bewildered loser who knew exactly what was happening to him, and also realised that, for the first time in his life, he just wasn't going to have enough time to protest about it.

And then it happened.

A second report, as if punctuating Garrity's hopelessness. I bellowed, '*Down*, Garrity . . . !' as the first parted length of wire buzz-sawed skywards, screeching through the sparking, smoking derrick-head block in a crazily gyrating, gleaming flash of blurring movement. Garrity started to dodge sideways, falling out of the seat towards the protection of the deck just as the so-skilfully fashioned patch began to carry away too, trailing the still-airborne winch wire after it in a monstrous, momentum-gathering plunge towards the sea.

Somebody sobbed '*Christ!*' from the upper deck and I never found out whether it was a prayer for Garrity or for the blood, sweat and curses which had gone into the creation of that tumbling juggernaut.

Suddenly it slammed to a halt in its downward path, held momentarily by the one thrumming derrick in a wallowing, pendulum orbit. Then the topping lift of the derrick itself carried away under the dead weight and the whole rig collapsed over the side in a booming, avalanching horror of steel and splintering wood and screeching, flailing wire rope . . .

While the note of Garrity's winch motor, still under full reverse power, rose to a new high as the inboard end of the release wire came lashing back towards its source. I watched three-inch thick hatch boards jumping frenziedly as the supersonic cheese-cutter carved a path clean through them, buzzing all the time like a demented bluebottle, then whipping low along the rolling deck to home on the screaming, runaway winch.

And then the screaming stopped because it hadn't been the winch screaming anyway, and the high-tensile serpent had coiled around Garrity and lifted him and the bucket seat and most of the control panel clean over the port side of the *Sarikamis*, leaving only a little piece of an arm and a hand to prove he'd ever been on board at all.

It was extraordinarily peaceful, lying there on the deck.

Now that the wave, and the patch – and Rigger Garrity – had gone.

It was quite a long time later that I found out why the wire really had parted.

Someone had cut through some of the outer strands with a file. The scratches were easily visible to the naked eye.

Probably we would have lost the patch even if the weather had been a flat calm.

The real irony was that we might also have lost most of our salvage crew – if the *Tsunami* hadn't saved them by forcing us to clear the danger area a few minutes early.

The following morning I bumped into John as I climbed the ladder to the boat deck. He was eating a bacon sandwich and looked a bit pleased with himself. I wondered whether to tell him about the deliberately sabotaged wire and then decided not to. It didn't make a lot of difference now and, anyway, we'd already gone over the pros and cons of sending our guests ashore so many times before.

And I wasn't even sure about *them* any more. Not after
watching Lenz's performance in the face of that ironically
opportune *Tsunami*. But I wasn't entirely in my dotage yet
– while there was still the enigmatic and elegant Tilsley to
figure. And that high-tension Burak kid. In fact *especially*
Third Officer Rifat Burak . . .

I said wearily, 'Who's on the poop? Watching the stern
lines?'

John threw the crust overboard and wiped his fingers.
'Some of the shipwrights. They have to replace the chafing
pads anyway and I'll go along later, before dark . . .' He
hesitated. 'Well. Aren't you going to ask me? About the
patch?'

One glance forward, over the flayed foredeck with the
slashed hatch cover and two or three riggers still sawing
gloomily to clear away the tangled spirals of broken wire. I
didn't see much point in it but I asked anyway. Just to keep
him happy.

'What about the patch?'

He lit a cigarette and handed it to me, fumbling for
another one. 'It's O.K. Good as new. Mike Tracey's boys have
just found it.'

I looked at him, hardly daring to hope. 'On the bottom.
And undamaged?'

'There's half a bent derrick lying across it, and it's wrapped
in wire like a Christmas parcel, but otherwise . . . well, we can
still use it. Maybe by tomorrow morning, once we get the
forward handling gear rigged again. And if the weather
eases.'

I started to smile as, all of a sudden the world didn't seem
such a bad place to be aboard after all. Then I stopped
grinning. 'And what about Garrity? Have they found him
too?'

John bit his lip. 'Quite a lot of him. There's a lot of wire
over and around . . .' He shrugged and brightened again.

'Let's take a look on the bridge, huh? And then get some sleep in before tonight.'

There wasn't a lot to see though. It was just an ordinary, well-appointed ship's bridge – apart from the last chart used during the approach into this bay. And on that, quite plainly and without any attempt to conceal or erase it, was marked the last courseline of the *Sarikamis*'s abruptly terminated voyage.

Leading straight towards, and vanishing into, the cliffs of Ras oum Achiche.

A spectacle case lay beside it, almost as though the navigator laying off that course had unconsciously placed it in the same spot he'd used on many, many previous occasions. There was a label, white against the tooled red Morocco skin, marked in both English and Turkish characters.

It said unequivocally – CAPTAIN SEVKET KOROGLU.

The gale was still blowing hard as we arrived at the bottom of the bridge ladders again. The boat deck – looking strangely forlorn with its empty lifeboat cradles and the idle, curved davits leaning out and still waiting patiently for boats to return which never would – seemed to magnify the force of the wind, catching it and whirling it into miniature tornados which caught the tapes of abandoned lifejackets and jerseys and the odd seaboots, probably kicked off by some panic-stricken owner who'd been optimistic enough to think he could at least swim for it if the boat went over . . .

John sniffed, shivering. 'It's getting worse. I'll take another look aft at the stern anchors.'

I glanced at him. He was starting to look really ill as the strain and fatigue took its toll. 'Leave it, Johnny. You go down and sleep, I've already had a spell below. I'll check out the poop. And there's not much we can do about the patch until the weather eases.'

He looked at me anxiously. 'Look, I *was* right, wasn't I . . . about flooding her by the head so's she'd grip harder? Even if it does make it more difficult to haul her off.'

I nodded. 'Sure. If you hadn't she'd be tearing the whole

bottom out've herself by now, under this swell. Now – shove off, chum. Get your head down!'

John smiled wistfully. 'It's going to be so nice, Peter. Spending that salvage award on *Tactician*.'

I watched him go, staggering slightly under the influence both of the ship's motion and sheer fatigue. I hoped he was right about the money. But I hadn't told him about that sabotaged wire, and that suggested we still had a lot more than a salvage problem to fight. Because the dead Captain Koroglu sure as hell couldn't have known we'd be using that particular cargo-handling gear to save the ship he'd so incomprehensibly tried to wreck. I mean, a dead man just can't file a wire rope half way . . .

I stopped, staring at the nearest empty davit – number one boat. The Captain's boat. The boat which I'd actually seen upending before it even reached the water . . . because *its* wire-rope after falls had parted – just like the derrick last night . . .

Urgently I hauled the greased wire inboard, leaning out over the white foam that surged angrily against the side of the ship fifty feet below. Heaving the dangling broken fall up hand over hand until I'd recovered the frayed, already salt-dulled end.

The scratches surrounding it were still shiny, though.

Where a file had eased all the strength out of it. Only there hadn't been a *Tsunami* to save the Captain!

CHAPTER TEN

I told them not to call John until midnight and, when he finally came aft to relieve me, he looked a lot better, much more like the old John I knew.

He looked a bit less cheerful when he reached the top of the poop deck ladder though, when – before I could warn him – a green sea came right in over the counter and very nearly washed him all the way back to midships again.

He growled irritably, 'Aaaah . . . *bloody* boats.' While I stuck my head cautiously around the crew's galley door and said, 'If you've had your bath maybe you'd like to let me go to bed, huh?'

The stern heaved again as another breaker burst under us, exploding in a roaring column of near-solid spray. The wind had come at last – the real wind – howling down from the north west and virtually shaking the *Sarikamis* like a rag doll with the rage of it. But also in spiteful frustration for it knew that, even allied to the seas which now climbed occasionally above the very rails themselves, it couldn't live long enough to tear us loose from the Scab.

Because there was another killer loose in the Northern Mediterranean now. But this was a friendly killer, if you happened to be a sailor. It even advertised its presence – the weather forecast we'd received two hours ago told me about it. That it would announce its arrival by the movement of a barometer needle, and that its name was *Anticyclone* . . . and that it would smother the breath of our gale very shortly.

Perhaps by early morning. And then we could save the *Sarikamis*.

It wouldn't matter then about missing detonators, or sabotaged wires or mysteries which didn't seem to have any logical solution. At this moment the sea helped to protect us in one way by its violence – because no one would attempt to arm a mine when there wasn't a hope in hell of them leaving before it blew them, as well as the *Sarikamis*, apart. And I personally intended to check every last inch of any new lifting wires already prepared by our riggers for tomorrow's final patching operation.

While for the next few hours a damp, but very aggressive John Templeton, would make quite sure that the same sinister threat which still tangibly overshadowed the ship, would have no opportunity to assist the final assault of the gale by releasing the anchor lines now in his care.

So I said fondly, 'Night, Johnny,' and left him huddled over the red-hot galley stove, sliding cheerfully down the ladder to the well deck before another sea could sneak up on me. It was almost like being back to normal again. A watch completed, a snug bunk waiting for me, and plenty of tea and sandwiches laid on if I wanted to spend a few minutes in dreaming of just how we were going to spend Lloyd's salvage award.

Until, just as I reached a point abreast of number six hatch, now canvased over to guard against a sneak sea, a flash of light caught my eye. It came from the far corner, where someone had carelessly left the forward edge of the hatch cover folded back.

Except that it wasn't carelessness. Because someone was still down there, moving about in the lower 'tween deck with a suspiciously shaded torch. But it was only when I walked quietly over, and stared down into the hold, that I also realised something else. Something very, very frightening indeed.

That I was now gazing into the compartment containing two hundred Amatol-packed sea mines!

The mines lay below me, gleaming softly as they reflected the light from the shaded torch. Martial ranks of black, evil spheres fading into the darkness of the hold, each with its protruding horns like the feelers of some threatening, hideous crustacean sea creature temporarily stranded from its natural element.

The shadowy, anonymous figure holding the torch seemed to be examining, rather than interfering, with this particular cargo. Which was O.K. by me as long as whoever it was didn't get a sudden urge to experiment a little. He appeared, in fact, to be especially interested in the first two mines in the double column along the starboard side because the pencil of light played for quite a long time over the black painted surfaces before it finally flicked off and the still unidentifiable intruder turned towards the ladder.

Quickly I drew back, searching anxiously for a hiding place. For a brief moment I wondered whether to call John, then I decided to wait a little longer. Right then the one obsessive interest I had was to identify that nocturnal investigator who appeared to count sea mines instead of sheep in the middle of the night.

Peering rather self-consciously round the cover of the mainmast I watched as the head rose above the level of the hatch cover, gazed cautiously around the deserted deck, then quickly scrambled over the coaming and replaced the canvas. For a moment he seemed to hesitate, looking aft towards the shaft of light from the open galley door, then abruptly the figure turned and moved silently past me, heading for the midships accommodation.

As he came abreast I saw he was a big man, a very familiar man. But the expression on the weatherbeaten features wasn't quite as I could ever remember seeing it before. It was thoughtful, grim, and almost guilty in an apprehensive kind of way.

It seemed to change him completely, to make him a suddenly foreign, inexplicable stranger. Yet I still couldn't bring myself to accept it. Not just like that.

Not with Tanker. One of the two men I respected more than anyone else in the world.

And then our Bosun had gone, moving surreptitiously along the starboard centrecastle alleyway and vanishing forward. For a moment I thought of following him, having the whole thing out right away, but there was one other compelling urge to satisfy first. So I moved somewhat apprehensively towards number six after hatch.

And climbed gingerly into the hold. Amongst those shadowy, globular horrors which waited so patiently in formation.

But there wasn't really anything to see. Just the mines blinking enigmatically back at me with their soft metal feelers and the oval, bolt-studded plate like a surprised mouth which was actually the cover for the arming devices – and I didn't exactly want to mess around with *that* particular feature. And anyway, unless someone intended to hit one with a hammer there was certainly no evidence of any delayed action triggering device in number six lower 'tween decks at that particular time.

I turned away thoughtfully, asking myself over and over again *why* Tanker had been down here. Had he been actually doing something . . . or just looking for something? And then I hesitated with one hand on the rung of the ladder as a barely noticed, perhaps irrelevant, detail flickered into focus in my over-active mind.

Turning back I gingerly moved amongst the dark spheres again, examining each one of maybe the first twenty in the rank for that single, curiously worrying detail which had so nearly escaped my notice.

Then I went back to the right-hand mine of the leading pair – the two secured nearest to the square of the hatch – and squatted down beside it, staring blankly at the one innocuous feature which apparently distinguished it from one hundred and ninety-nine brothers.

A little green-painted symbol, less than half an inch high and shaped like a curly-tailed tadpole, situated just under the turn of the steel elliptical cover which waterproofed the arming compartment.

It was an eerie, spine-chilling sensation. Sitting there in the dark and listening to the sea rushing and drumming and booming against the outer skin of an otherwise, silent, dead ship.

And just staring incomprehendingly. At that odd mine out.

Perhaps I should have told John then, but I don't think it would have made any difference in the end. And he already had a lot on his mind, because he was the real salvage expert of our team. I was just a specialist at pulling and lifting inanimate objects which didn't want to be pulled and lifted. It would be John who would save the *Sarikamis* and I didn't want to add any further strain to his already aggravated technical problems.

So *I* opened the cover of that one mine with a tadpole-shaped personality. Oh, common sense told me nothing could happen – not just unscrewing a few nuts on a steel plate. But by the time I'd removed the last one using the adjustable spanner from my sheath I could feel the cold sweat trickling unashamedly into my eyes.

What really kept me turning was the promise I made to myself – that if this one blew, I'd never touch another bloody sea mine again.

Then ever so carefully I prised up the edge of the plate, and peered apprehensively inside. And saw nothing.

Or to be strictly accurate, I did see the oblong recess where I assumed the dry battery required to make the electrical firing circuits would normally be inserted. And the shiny-brass threaded housing to hold the detonator and primer. But they were all empty and reflecting only the beam of my torch from lightly oiled surfaces.

It was all a bit anti-climactic, really. To find that my singularly outstanding menace was completely harmless. And that I still hadn't found the missing detonator after all that.

I did notice, as I replaced the cover, how little of the inside of the mine was seen through the arming compartment. I remembered reading once, though, that the greater part of a contact mine is occupied by the explosive filling plus air space to give the required buoyancy and allow it to float suspended above its sinker . . . and I didn't really want to examine a quarter of a ton of Amatol anyway, not even if it was as safe as Plasticine in its present state.

It was only when I'd finally climbed out of the hatch, and had replaced the cover with an overwhelming sense of relief, that I first saw the dim figure moving surreptitiously aft towards the poop where John still presumably guarded the stern anchor wires.

I thought bitterly, 'Oh, not *again* f'r cryin' out lou . . .' when the heaviest sea yet slammed in under our quarter, literally climbed right up over the taffrail and came surging over the break of the poop in a roaring avalanche of foam.

For a moment the intruder clung to the ladder, fighting to hold his grip against the sea. It struck me then that, if the weather worsened any more, the after end of the *Sarikamis* would be untenable, the raised poop an inaccessible island cut off from the centrecastle by a sea-scoured well deck . . .

. . . and God help us then if those after wires parted and she was free to swing broadside to the Scab.

I watched that drenched, still unidentifiable man struggle doggedly upwards against the last of the draining torrent and suddenly thought about John, snugly unaware in the galley space where I'd left him earlier. And I knew I had to warn him because, whatever else, that nocturnal visitor was moving with a surreptitious air that indicated only a threat to the safety of the *Sarikamis*. And to John Templeton.

Until, suddenly, everything seemed to happen all at once.

The door of the galley opened abruptly – maybe John had decided to check on the results of that last, pounding blow – then I saw my partner appear round the side of the deck-housing and stop as he came virtually face to face with the intruder.

126

I heard his outraged bellow. 'What the *bloody* . . . ?'

Just before, with a high-pitched shriek of absolute terror, that dripping, outrageous trespasser turned and literally fled back down the ladder pursued by an equally astonished and disconcerted John. It was all so weird and unexpected that, for a moment, I could only stand and gape as the two galloping figures zoomed past me, racing along the opposite side of the hatch and disappearing forward with two pairs of feet throwing great splashes of water like winged hooves of mythology.

In fact I only had time to see, as the arc of a gyrating cargo cluster sparked across the fleeing man's face, that I was looking at the almost maniacally staring eyes of the kid called Burak, currently Third Officer of the Motor Vessel *Sarikamis*.

And then I started to move too, intending to head the apparently crazed young Mate off before he could reach the forward decks . . .

. . . until something hard and heavy hit me across the base of my skull, and I'd only time to remember for a very brief moment that now there wasn't anyone left to guard those bloody stern anchor wires – before I couldn't remember anything else at all . . .

Someone poured a thousand gallons of icy water over me and I spluttered weakly, 'Okay, *okay*! I'll be up on the bridge in a min . . .'

Then another few tons of sea came waltzing across the deck and I felt myself rolling and drowning and being battered to death all at the same time, which was a bit bloody much just 'cause a bloke's slept past the time to relieve the watch . . .

. . . until my feet fell away from under me and I tried to stare at the water-distorted orbs of the cargo lamps above before I realised, with a howl of undiluted terror, that a huge sea had swamped inboard over the starboard bulwarks and that I was now hanging half in and half out of the freeing ports along the port scuppers, jammed by the hinged steel flap which trapped my thighs.

And that one more wave would spit me over the wall like a bullet from an aqua-gun.

From a long way away someone was roaring 'Skipper! Hold *on*, Skipper!' and it sounded a bit like Tanker's voice, only it couldn't be because he was down in number six hold trying to arrange a Fifth of November send-off for the little bit of North Africa around the *Sarikamis* . . . or was that yesterday? And had Tanker actually *done* anything to my tadpole . . . my little, green, secret tadpole on a mine . . .

Then his huge paw was gripping my collar just like it had done that time aboard the capsizing *Vespasian*, and another sea fell on top of us, and another . . . and I thought hysterically, 'Hanging around like this could get to be a bloody career . . .'

Until he finally gave a great heave which seemed to separate my legs from my pelvis, and I screamed 'Oh *Je*suuuuuus!' in agony as I felt him dragging me over every sea-washed ring bolt between us and the comparative security of the centre-castle overhang. But then I didn't have any more time for pain because Tanker's face hung over me with a look of terrible concern, and roared, 'You better be ready to give the order, Skipper. Before she hits . . .

. . . to abandon ship!'

I remember glancing stupidly at my watch and noticing the time was just after one a.m. It meant I'd been unconscious for three quarters of an hour, and the excruciating ache under my ear told me why. I should, by rights, have been dead already with a blow like that – though as far as I could make out from the expression on Tanker's features that detail would only be a brief question of time anyway.

The well deck was literally seething with rampaging water. Even as I watched another sea collapsed inboard with the spray climbing in a great slow column as it atomised against the hatch coamings and the mainmast housing. Right aft all I could make out was the dim bulk of the poop, now completely cut off from us as the ship rolled more and more violently.

And there was only one thing which could make her roll like that.

I said sickly, 'The st'b'd quarter hook's gone, hasn't it? We're already swinging broadside to the weather!'

Behind me I suddenly became aware of the rest of the men but I couldn't see John among them. Though why in God's name wasn't he here . . . ? I tried to ask, but no one seemed to know — and anyway, they all had their own problems.

One of the shipwrights said hopefully, 'There's the inflatables. Maybe we can ride it out in them, Skipper.'

And someone else, obviously a seaman, spat contemptuously. We all knew what he meant — we'd all seen what had happened to the last men to abandon the *Sarikamis*.

Tanker gestured at the white water between us and the stern. 'I'm goin' to have a go at getting through. I already called *Tactician* an' told Barney to bring her in close, try shooting a line when I gives him a flash.'

Yet another breaker pummelled the hull under us. The group winced as nearly solid water slashed across exposed faces and someone started to cry. Quietly, and not so much with fear as with resignation. And maybe just a little bit of regret . . . I saw it was the young lad who'd found McKay's mutilated corpse and felt very sad.

Swallowing hard I tried to fight the nausea which suggested I was still in shock from the attack on me, and the subsequent battering I'd received from the sea. 'You really think *Tactician* could hold her off the reef, Tanker? Even if we could pass the tow?'

He grinned. 'If she can't I'll personally jump over the bloody wall.'

I didn't smile back. 'If she can't, boyo, we'll *all* have to jump over the bloody wall . . . But it's no damn good, Bosun — nobody can get through that water. We can't even take the rocket line inboard, never mind the towing hawser.'

'Yeah, Well, maybe not, Skipper.' He wasn't grinning any more either. Not now. 'But by *God* I'm goin' to try!'

The *Sarikamis* heaved like a wounded animal. Even here, far from the bows, I could hear the agony of tortured metal and I knew it wouldn't be very long now. And whichever way we went over the side, in that sea it wouldn't make any difference . . . I said wearily, 'Okay. But we tie a rope between us. I'm going with you.'

The huge bulk of a man pushed forward through the crowd.

'*Nein!*'

I thought weakly, 'Oh Jesus, but can't the bloody Germans ever say anythin' except Nine?'

Lenz shook his cropped skull like a gimballed globe of the moon, all white and pasty. 'You will be a drawback, Herr Rose. Your Bosun will have to drag you also through the water . . .'

I whirled on him, feeling the hysteria mounting. Now not only did I have to go and commit a particularly horrific form of suicide, but I was also expected to argue about getting the privilege. I snarled viciously, '*Tough*, Lenz! So shut your big flabby mouth an' take a runni . . .'

He said simply, 'I will go instead, *Kapitan*. I am the only other man aboard this ship who has the *Widerstandsfähigkeit* . . . the strong body, *hein?*'

'I'm going too.'

I turned again. Tilsley was standing white-faced but looking very, very determined. I noticed distantly that the fancy Gieves' uniform had been replaced by a rather more practical white seaman's jersey, but it wasn't really the time for fashion notes.

'Oh, good, . . .' I said bitterly. 'Now everyone wants to be a hero.'

The ship reared again and I could see Tilsley's eyes staring almost hypnotically over my shoulder, watching that half-submerged, inmpossible island where the tow would have to be made fast – even if they ever made it in the first place. And *then* managed to manhandle an outrageous weight of water-sodden line to the warping winch in order to bring the deadweight of the final towing wire aboard once again . . .

'I want to go too, Ross,' he snapped tightly. 'Dammit man, I've got to. She's my ship, don't forget!'

Just for a moment I stared at him in surprise. And feeling even more confused than ever – because if *Tilsley* was so damn keen to save the *Sarikamis*, and Lenz had already proved on several occasions that he and the Menteses undoubtedly intended to – then who else was left to carry the guilt of running her aground?

Apart from her long-dead Captain who could still, apparently, file wire ropes in half and cast off lines from the poop in the middle of the night?

Or *Burak*!

Third Officer Burak. That young kid who couldn't even stand up to a surprise confrontation with John Templeton without running like a startled fawn . . . And that made me think about John, too. While the sick feeling of despair came surging back because I knew that, whoever else should have been here among this group of miserable, shivering seamen, John certainly would have been.

If he was *able* to . . .

Tanker was already securing the bight of a line around Lenz's enormous girth. He caught my eye and I could see he was worried about the time we had left. The ship was already broadsiding and, now the swing had started, she would just keep on going . . . I shook my head at Tilsley. 'Two men only. Tanker and Lenz. But they'll take the end of the rope with them and secure it aft. Then the rest of us can use it as a lifeline.'

The Chief Officer's eyes bored into mine with an almost

frantic desperation yet, ironically, I also knew Tilsley was frightened. Too frightened to be anything other than a liability out there on that exposed well deck – so what was really driving him to volunteer? None of us had much of a chance of survival either way, but the men who went out there had even less. If they lost their footing they'd be dead before they even went over the side, smashed out of recognition against the forest of steel projections surmounting a ship's deck.

'Two men only, Tilsley. We follow when we can.'

Tanker finished the bowline around his own waist and made the other end fast to the ladder beside me. Tilsley seemed to hesitate even then, until he swung away abruptly and stared grim-faced out to where *Tactician*'s steaming lights occasionally appeared, gyrating crazily through cotton-wool clouds of spray, as she closed our stern. I hoped Barney wouldn't come in too close, not like John had done that time with the *Vespasian* . . . and that started me worrying about John's disappearance again.

And the even more chilling absence of Third Officer Rifat Burak.

Just for a moment the two huge Bosuns gazed at each other silently. The British seaman and the German – what? But I saw there was a certain respect in that look, and also a mutual wariness, almost like two rogue elephants who meet before doing battle. Then Tanker gave a savage grin and jerked his head towards the poop.

'C'mon in, Lenz . . . the water's fine.'

And they'd gone. With only the tenuous umbilical cord of that slowly uncoiling line to show they'd ever been with us at all.

But she was a demanding ship, the *Sarikamis*. An avaricious, greedy ship. When she gave, under duress, she gave grudgingly and only then after the price had been paid in full. As it had been by those drowned, floating part-sailors from the capsized orange boats, and by McKay who didn't have any back to his head. And by stubborn, bloody-minded Rigger Garrity who still lay below us cocooned in a steel wire shroud.

So it wasn't too much of a surprise to find that she was still a wilful bitch with a leaning towards self-destruction. And in order to persuade her to delay her suicidal advances in the face of the Scab's beckoning, we would have to be prepared to pay yet another ransom.

Which she claimed with spiteful contempt. Before she would even allow us to try and take *Tactician*'s first slender line aboard.

I actually watched him go, plucked hugely from the lifeline beside me and hurled sickeningly against the port ladder where he clung desperately, staring at the next sea rearing above us until it collapsed inboard in a raging, swirling cataract. And then I heard his shrill voice above the roar of the water – 'Help me, Skipper! For God's sake . . . please help meeeee*eeee*!'

Then he wasn't there any more, the young boy from *Tactician*. Only the bloody smears from the tips of torn, scrabbling fingers slowly splaying against the white paint of the handrail before yet another sea hosed them away too, and left the rest of us floundering in a choking, helpless string, spaced along the safety line like a long row of codfish suspended on a deep sea cast.

Until the Herculean Lenz, one huge paw anchored firmly to a stay, dragged the rest of us one by one under the break of the poop and with shocked, dull faces we scrambled towards the taffrail where Tanker was already flashing Barney to come in and shoot.

I gasped, 'The kid's gone over the wall,' and Tanker said absently, 'He'd've been a good boy, that . . . WATCH *OUT* f'r the thrower there!' then we all clung to the taffrail, leaning into the gale with the black sea rearing up at us and the spray slashing horizontally as the last throes of the doomed wind flailed us with a terrible hate.

An image of the tug hands braced on *Tactician*'s after deck, almost under us with the Schermuly pistol angled upwards and to windward, leading line flaked down ready to follow its rocket . . . and on to that light line was already bent a heavier nylon rope, then a wire and, finally, the tow itself.

If we could even catch the leader in the first place. And then pull together on a waterlogged, ice-rink deck which wouldn't keep still for long enough to catch your balance.

Maybe forty-five degrees off the wind now. Roughly half-way round from the *Sarikamis*'s original right angle to the reef, and broaching-to fast. Broadsiding with the windward seas piling in furious welters of foam as high as the well deck bulwarks while, on our lee side, a slowly undulating nothing-ness which only became a horror once again as it thundered sullenly along the length of the slowly closing Scab.

Slam!

A tail of fire, red and white with the pink-reflecting line chasing behind in a long, whipping snake . . . and the gale snatching it in a wide curving arc before drowning it in the sea fifty feet to our right.

A snarl from the grim line of men. 'Cloth brained bastard!'

Someone else. Unbelievably resentful. 'Calls hisself a bloody seaman. Couldn't put it in a whore's . . .' The spume came again, screaming with mockery. '. . . not even with effin' floodlights!'

Feverish activity on *Tactician*'s deck. Bending on the second line. The masthead lamp below us soared through eighty degrees and I watched in raging, helpless frustration as one yellow-oilskinned figure tumbled helter-skelter in a flail-ing, bone-shaking slide.

Slam again!

The line right above us this time but veering fast to leeward.

'HOLD it! Aw f'r *Chris* . . .'

The man at the very end of our group standing as if paralysed, the line literally sailing down across his shoulders and him not doing a *bloody* thing to catch it. The whole crowd surging across towards him with outstretched, clutching hands . . . 'Get a *grip*, damn you!'

A glimpse of the statue's face, staring down at the white nylon thread over him with the dead expression of an abruptly switched off robot. Fear? Incredulity? Exposure dulling already overtaxed reflexes . . . ? I didn't really think so.

Not when the frozen man was a rather competent Chief Officer. And Tilsley was anything but slow on the uptake!

But then Lenz and Tanker buried him together, hurling their huge forms towards him and leaving him dazed with the shocking impact of it while the line, now secure in horny, agile hands, started to come aboard smooth as the nylon it was made of.

And then the rope. And the wire. Manhandled over to the already slowly revolving warping winch. And finally the tow, rising dripping and surging in a great, hanging bight out of the gale-torn sea.

I watched nervously as *Tactician* gradually took the strain, veering in a wide arc until she was steaming virtually at right angles to the length of the *Sarikamis* with her bluff bows parting the seas in wide-flung gouts of white water. That knot of helpless frustration tightened into a burning pain as I stood there wishing desperately that it was me, and not Barney Slough over there on *Tactician*'s tiny bridge, because holding an eight thousand ton freighter against this kind of wind was a job for an experienced tugboat man, and not for someone with a lot of theory and not very much practice . . .

And then Tanker yelled, 'He's got her, Skipper. By Jiminy but he's holdin' her!' and I felt just a little bit resentful because it really *should've* needed an expert like me – or maybe Barney was just lucky for once. Then I realised some people were even luckier than Barney, and that I was one of them, just as the crowd of saturated salvage men on the *Sarikamis*'s poop started to whistle and shout and slap each other on the back like a bunch of schoolkids on a picnic outing.

I also noticed the way the two men who'd really saved us were looking at each other. There was an even more marked respect in that glance which passed between the English and the German Bosun . . . but also that other indefinable understanding. That they would pit their strength and wits yet again. But maybe, next time, on different sides of an equally nebulous fence.

Tilsley was still sprawled, winded, on the streaming deck. Painfully he stretched a wavering arm towards Lenz for support, but the big German just gazed back down at him with . . . I wasn't quite sure . . . was it contempt? Or was it something even deeper? Something that Lenz had suddenly found out about Tilsley that I hadn't?

And then Lenz quite deliberately turned away and was critically examining the tow where it was secured to the poop. Tanker noticed the strange incident as well, but he too stared pointedly down at the groping Chief Officer with a grin big enough to swallow a melon.

'If you can't take a joke, you shouldn't've joined, Mister,' he said cheerfully. And then he also turned his broad back on the white-faced Mate of the *Sarikamis*.

But I had too much on my mind for relieved comedy. This time I had to know.

'Anyone seen Mister Templeton?' I called anxiously.

There was a sudden silence on the poop as the excited laughter died away and the men came back to the reality of the *Sarikamis*'s unspeakable menace. Tanker whirled round, his red sweating face grim. 'You mean he's not with us? But dammit, he was on watch up here, Skip . . .'

Then it hit him, the realisation of what he'd just said. There was an uneasy shuffling from the crowd and I saw men glancing meaningfully at each other while a faint bell tinkled in my mind. Only I was too worried, too frightened for

John to realise the consequences of saying the wrong thing. So stupidly I muttered, 'Yeah! And the last time that line was sabotaged McKay got his skull smashed in — so where is Mister Templeton, Bosun . . . and Burak?'

'Burak's sick, Ross. Sick in the head . . .'

I swung on Tilsley, now holding painfully on to the rail with the look of a resentful man in his salt-burned eyes. 'What d'you mean, Tilsley — sick?'

'He's unbalanced, liable to do anything. I dunno . . . maybe he even had something to do with the wrecking of this bloody hulk in the first place. Like I said, he was on Koroglu's watch entering the bay, and we only have his word that he was sent below.'

There was a mutter from the men and I started to get scared. The atmosphere on the poop had suddenly changed from one of relief to one of nerve-taut hysteria. Mob hysteria. I'd only seen a similar phenomenon once before when, as a cadet, my ship had been moored alongside a beat-up old Shanghai freighter. Apparently one of her sailors had been caught red-handed at the end of a long series of crew thefts.

And they'd lynched that man. They'd dragged him out on the after deck of that rusted freighter, thrown a steel-wire cargo sling around the screaming man's neck, and hoisted him aloft with a clanking, rattling old steam winch . . .

I said desperately, 'The hell with Burak! I want Mister Templeton found . . .'

Someone yelled from the back, 'I seen him. Maybe an hour ago. Runnin' forward jus' before the ship started to broach to.'

Tanker jerked his head quickly. 'Right! Get looking . . .'

The anonymous voice snarled aggressively, 'I din't say I was finished, Bosun . . . Mister T was chasing someone. Goin' like the clappers.'

I thought sickly, 'Oh God but that's *it*.'

Rifat. Ras oum Achi*che*.'

I drew a deep breath. '*You* made that VHF Mayday call, didn't you, Burak? More than three hours before this ship actually grounded.'

Tanker moved in menacingly behind me. I hoped he wouldn't lose his head and go for the kid but I didn't dare say anything right then which might have broken the mood.

For a moment the boy in the stained reefer jacket only stared hopelessly at the two of us. Then he said, quite simply, 'I was very frightened. These cliffs – at full speed? So I sneak into the wheelhouse and make the VHF message while my partner not know . . . !'

I whispered softly, 'And your partner, Rifat. Who was your partner. Who really was responsible for wrecking the *Sarikamis*?'

But it was all too much for Tanker. Roaring like an enraged bull he made a grab at the slim figure before us. 'So it was *you* killed all those poor bloody sailormen, Burak. You knew they was goin' to get the deep six, you little bastard!'

I shouted desperately, 'NO, Tanker! He's going to talk, man. To tell us who else is involved . . .'

Only I was too late. Far too late. The kid gave a last, almost girlish shriek of sheer terror and darted for the now unguarded door, twisting like a greased eel under Tanker's outstretched hand. Then he was gone, lost in the starboard centrecastle alleyways before we could even reach the deck.

I glared at Tanker, too sick to even speak. He had the grace to look guilty, and shuffled awkwardly. 'Sorry, Skipper,' he muttered, 'It was jus' thinkin' about all them drowned sailormen.'

We moved silently aft, pushing angrily through the knots of violent men still searching for a victim. I knew someone else would find Burak again. It was only a question of whether he would still be fit to talk by the time I could get to him for a second attempt at solving the mystery.

It was only when we reached the after deck and I saw number six hatch that I remembered those bloody awful mines we still carried. And they, in turn, made me think about Tanker's surreptitious nocturnal visit to the hold. And the faintly worrying understanding there seemed to be between him and the incomprehensible German, Lenz.

And *that* – in its turn – made me wonder if he genuinely had cut Burak's confession short out of anger over a beachful of dead men.

Or could it have been because even Tanker didn't want me to know just why those same men had really died?

We didn't find John, or any trace of him. But we did find Burak again, as I knew we would.

Only he was a long way from where I could help him this time. Because I was still on the lower cargo decks when the frail figure of the kid next appeared. Sixty feet above me, right on the wheelhouse roof.

And he wasn't alone either – because now he had Lenz and the chilling Brothers Mentese for company.

I remember the hopelessness of those moments after Burak had disappeared. Standing there on that windswept after deck and seeing the dawn light pushing a yellow probe above the horizon while, all the time, men prowled and searched and swore as the first flush of hysteria wore away to be replaced by disappointment and fatigue. But they were still dangerous. Still too tautly wound to try to reason with. Only I also realised that, while they wanted Burak so viciously, they were covering the ship in search of John.

So I didn't even try and stop them. I just stood there thinking about Tanker's secret, and John, and remembering that time on the boat deck when he'd turned to face me before he went below. And he'd said so happily, 'It's going to be nice, Peter. Spending that salvage award on *Tactician*.'

Tanker scratched his head and looked sideways at me. He

seemed worried and embarrassed. 'Sorry about that mistake with the kid, Skipper. I'm a stupid bastard an' that's a fact.'

I stared at him for a moment, and wondered just how well I really knew the man I'd sailed with for such a long time. Then I said quietly, 'Are you, Tanker?'

And walked away.

But I'd only just arrived on the forward deck again when one of the salvage crew shouted in a hushed voice, 'Jesus, look up there!' and I'd followed the abruptly craning necks higer and higher, climbing the sheer face of the centrecastle, up past the boat deck and bridge to the wheelhouse itself.

To see Third Officer Rifat Burak. Standing poised and terrified, with his back to a sixty foot drop!

An abrupt hush fell over the decks of the *Sarikamis*. It was an eerie, outlandish tableau right then, with groups of suddenly still men all gazing upwards with the swinging circles of the cargo lamps throwing angled, craggy features into spasmodic relief while the only other movement was from the flickering orange flames of tar brands which some of them held in frozen hands.

An almost physical silence. The silence of dead men aboard a dead, mutilated ship. But I sensed that, already, several of our salvage crew were showing signs of discomfort, that the mob was quickly dissolving into individual personalities once again, and a sort of embarrassed perplexity was taking the place of that horrifying mass hysteria.

Except with Lenz, and the two Menteses. Because the way they were closing on Burak up there high above us showed that there was still an unbridgable gulf between the salvage crew and the *Sarikamis* survivors. And, even from below, I could see that Lenz didn't feel a whisper of pity for the boy crouching, like a stag at bay, on the very edge of that sheer drop.

Someone moved up beside me. It was Tilsley. But he, too, was staring in taut anticipation at the scene above.

I roared urgently, 'Stay where you are, Lenz. The boy's

desperate. We'll coax him down easy, f'r God's sake!'

Only then The Brothers were moving in as well, circling round on three sides of the Third Officer in that menacing, reflex-tensed attitude of the professional knife fighter . . . and then I saw them — the blades. Flashing like diamonds under the glare of the lamps as the two Turkish deck hands almost casually tossed them from one hand to the other.

But, all the while slowly closing in.

It was nearly killing time once again, aboard the Motor Vessel *Sarikamis*.

Lenz took two quick, threatening steps towards the boy and the kid shrieked, just like he'd done that time earlier when Tanker had lunged for him. A sigh rose from the men around me, the kind of mass intake of breath a circus crowd utters as the high wire artiste sways unsteadily . . .

I felt the sweat running cold down the side of my nose. 'Call your boys off, Lenz . . . LENZ! You force him any further and it'll be murder, dammit! So help me I promise, Lenz — if the kid falls I'll put you an' the other two ashore on a charge of premeditated bloody murd . . .'

But then it happened anyway. Quite deliberately, and acting almost as if on a prearranged signal, the three grotesquely foreshortened figures made a last, violent rush towards Burak, compelling him backwards as if evading the pincers of some giant, nightmarish crab.

Only there wasn't any deck left to step back on to.

So the boy stumbled into space while the whimper grew to a disbelieving wail, and we stared in frozen horror as that slow-motion image of a gently revolving body grew larger and larger as it plummeted towards us . . .

. . . until abruptly the screaming cut dead while the hatch boards under my feet jumped under the impact. And Third Officer Rifat Burak sprawled in a bloody, shattered lump ten feet away from me.

While, from above, a coldly satisfied Teutonic voice called, 'We are ready to go ashore now, *Herr Kapitan*. Whenever it is convenient for bringing your tug alongside.'

I cradled the Third Officer's head in my arms. He was still alive when we reached him and I saw the looks of shock on the faces of the men around me. One expression I remember in particular – on Tilsley's white features. The *Sarikamis*'s Chief Officer was gazing down at his junior shipmate with an almost hypnotised stare and, just in that macabre fraction of time, I wondered whether there wasn't a little trace of apprehension in the nervous eyes – but was it in case Burak might die before we could save him . . . or *not* die before he could talk?

I remembered another striking coincidence, from back there on the poop before this tragic manhunt had started. That it had been Tilsley who had sown the first seeds of suspicion which had led to this. About Burak's possible involvement in the wrecking of the *Sarikamis*.

And then I forgot about Tilsley and everything else. When the bloodied, twisted lips moved with a terrible effort, and the thing which had been a youthful, handsome ship's officer croaked, 'Lenz . . . I have only now realised that he was sent to this ship to . . .'

The big black eyes flickered open and looked up at me with such a tired, lost expression. I knew he didn't have very much longer to suffer.

'Lenz, son . . . ?' I whispered while the ring of men above us stayed very quiet. '. . . what *about* Karl Lenz. And the Menteses?'

Now the fading voice was so distant I had to put my ear very close to the barely moving mouth. 'They were the men who were . . . responsible . . .'

Bright red blood, glinting with tiny bubbles of foam, trickled between the slack lips and ran over my arm. Gently I eased the poor head down against the rough canvas of the hatch cover and stood up. Rifat Burak was dead.

Lifting my eyes I saw Tanker watching me closely. Was he assessing my reactions, or just waiting to find out what came next? But I didn't care any more. Not about how much Tanker knew or didn't know. Or about why the *Sarikamis* had been wrecked, or about sabotaged wires and what had transformed ordinary, decent men into less than animals under the strain of being trapped in this horrible web.

I didn't even care now if I never found those missing detonators, or discovered the significance – if there ever had been any significance in the first place – in a green tadpole painted on a mine.

All I cared about now was John. And what had happened to him.

Because Burak had answered the only other really important question over the mystery of the *Sarikamis* tragedy – the identity of the man responsible for her near-destruction.

And, presumably, also responsible for everything which had happened since our arrival on board.

So Tilsley's yardarm was clear. I couldn't help feeling a little disappointed about that. But you can't condemn a man just because you don't like him.

'Lenz and the Menteses are to be locked in the sick bay, Tanker. They'll be sent ashore as soon as the weather eases enough to transfer them to *Tactician*. Understand?'

He nodded and I could see he felt a bit better to know I was at least talking to him again. 'An' if they don't fancy bein' locked up, Skipper?'

'Take four men with you. Give them a crowbar each . . .' I gazed at him bitterly, thinking about John. 'And, if there's any argument whatsover – just smash Lenzi's bloody skull in. Permanently!'

And then the rest of us started to search the crippled ship again. But in quiet concern, this time. Without hate.

CHAPTER ELEVEN

Twenty-four hours and the whimper of a dead gale later we still hadn't found any indication, not even a trace, of what had happened to John Templeton.

We'd literally searched that silent ship from truck to keel, men moving quietly and methodically through compartment after compartment, into store rooms still hung with provisions to make dinners for a dead and long gone crew, and through cabins which would never welcome their original inhabitants again.

I'd personally combed through that sinister, shadowed mine deck. Crawling over and round the menacing, regimental banks of spherical casings. But there was nothing there, apart from a chilling uneasy claustrophobia – and a tiny, meaningless green tadpole.

Johnny had gone. And the dreams with him. Because I'd never realised until then just how much he'd been a part of it all . . .

The threat had gone too. Or the triple threat which had shadowed the *Sarikamis* – in the gross shape of a riddle called Lenz, and the co-executioners Mentese. They'd gone as they'd previously remained – with a willingness which, by its very unexpectedness, had caused us to glance uneasily towards each other and frown, and to wonder why. And maybe to shiver just a little even though the sun had risen and the sea had eased temporarily to a gentle, undulating swell.

Tanker had sailed with them. He'd relieved Barney as soon as *Tactician* had recovered and re-laid that fateful starboard quarter anchor. Oh, I'd almost convinced myself I'd wanted to give him a break, to ease that strain which had become even more marked in him since John's inexplicable disappearance . . . but had that really been my motive? Or had I subconsciously wanted to remove Tanker as well – to rid the ship of the very last reminder of that nagging mystery which had haunted us since we first heard a radio plead *Mayday* . . . ?

Because I felt deep down that I couldn't afford to trust Tanker any more. Not after everything that had happened. Only I didn't have the guts – or was it the passion – to confront him with my suspicions. I was too tired and too worried, and too sick at heart. So I'd just growled brusquely, 'Take the tug into Djidjelli. Hand Lenz and Co. over and tell the police I want 'em here . . . and don't come back 'til you've got yourself good and drunk, Bosun – then be ready to haul this bastard until she either floats or her tail snaps off!'

And then I climbed wearily into a black rubber skin and went to examine a patch wrapped in wire at the bottom of the sea.

Only I found that I'd left one nightmare for another. Because all the time I was down there I kept visualising the fish-mutilated face of John Templeton – slug-white, with bulging eyes in a bloated mask and the soft hair reaching to the surface in accusing, restless tendrils from behind the yellow-green weed . . . a non-existent corpse under the bottom of that frightful ship I knew I still had to try and save.

Yet at the same time I also realised something else – that now the dream had vanished, I didn't really give a damn either way.

But I still had to keep on trying.

Because a lot of men had died already. And now I hated the *Sarikamis* far too much to let her destroy herself like she so desperately wanted to do.

Mike Tracey had to lean against the rail for a moment as he reached the deck. He pushed his diver's mask up to his forehead and I saw his face looked tired and drawn. The mask twinkled briefly as it caught the sun and, for a fraction of time, it looked as though he had a glass lid to his skull. Then he pushed himself upright and padded across the deck towards me.

'That's it, Skipper. All ready to go.'

I glanced at my watch – 10.15. By noon we would know if we could salvage the *Sarikamis*, or if we'd lost her forever. There was another gale on the way and, unless she refloated today, she wouldn't live through a second beating. Not without breaking her back on the Scab.

I said, 'How does it look, Mike?'

He shrugged. 'The hole's bigger. She must've opened up more when she broadsided that night. We've cut away the rough edges and the patch should still cover, but . . '

He shrugged again and I knew what he meant. We'd located the patch over the rent in the forward hold all right but, as that gash had enlarged, it conversely reduced the area of sound plating against which the patch would bear – and also reduced to a minimum the safety margin we'd allowed for when we started to pump out the internal water, and the outside pressure of the sea inexorably increased as it struggled to find its way around the man-made dam holding it at bay.

I was conscious of the men around me. All watching. Waiting for the word. It struck me then that, ever since that terrible man-hunt on the previous night, they'd driven themselves like demons, working with a fanatical energy which had left no room for food or sleep. Almost as though, by devoting themselves to saving the *Sarikamis*, they were in some small way absolving themselves from the part they'd indirectly played in Burak's shocking death.

A kind of masochistic penance. And maybe, like me, just a little bit of hate for the ship which had temporarily dragged them down to the level of animals.

Even Tilsley had worked, constantly urging and advising on ways to overcome the loss of the cargo gear when it had gone over the side that night, along with Rigger Garrity. But perhaps Tilsley, too, needed to reassure us – to underline the fact that he wasn't the same as Lenz and the Menteses. And that his loyalty was simply to his owners, as Chief Officer of their stranded ship.

Since the threat had gone he was certainly happier, I noticed that. And secretly relieved. In a not quite concealed kind of way.

I moved over to the hatch coaming and gazed down, following the corrugated lifting hoses of the six-inch pumps as they hung like great inverted caterpillars, head buried under the scum of water which rose almost to the level of the lower 'tween decks. There was still cargo down there too, under that gently undulating sea water, but if we could lower the level, and the patch held long enough, we could unload it as it became exposed and, finally, seal the whole length of the gash with cement.

If the patch held . . .

'Keep your divers clear of the indraft in case she implodes, Mike,' I said quietly. Then I gestured to Barney and raised my voice.

'Start the pumps, Mister. And open the lift valves!'

The *Sarikamis* seemed to shudder just a little. As if in silent protest.

The boat deck seemed more desolate than ever with its vacant lifeboat cradles and the gently swinging, empty falls. There wasn't even a wind, as there had been when I'd last stood up here with John, and now the flotsam scraps of rubbish left by a doomed crew lay still and pathetically forlorn in untidy little heaps.

It was lonely up there too, high above the sparkling sea with the shimmering golden sand spread out ahead of our bows and even the rocks of the Scab only revealing themselves by an occasional sullen swirl of white as each slow swell submerged them under an oily blanket.

Over to my left the distant cliffs of Ras oum Achiche rose in sheer majesty from the water, hardly recognisable now compared to that time so long ago when we'd watched a strange ship steam unbelievably towards them. And even further round the curve of the bay, far over to the east, the blue haze that marked Cape Bougaroni merged imperceptibly with the silver line of the horizon.

My eyes noted a faint break in the line, almost invisible. I wondered if it could be *Tactician* returning early from Djidjelli and, just for a moment, felt a surge of warm hope that it would be, and that Tanker would be with her. And then I remembered about John, and the cosy feeling vanished, leaving my stomach empty and tight again.

I glanced at my watch, half-listening to the steady roar of the pumps from the forward deck. 11.45. We'd been emptying the flooded hold for nearly ninety minutes now, watching tensely as the level of the water steadily dropped, but I hadn't been able to stay any longer – it had been like that ever since John had disappeared. I'd suddenly found myself wandering alone and always searching, hoping I would find him. Or some small, overlooked clue as to where he'd gone . . .

I glanced over the side, down towards the water. The inflatables rode like tethered dolphins, black and shining against the blue water around the base of the accommodation ladder. Further forward, nearly over the swirl of the Scab itself, the salvage pump discharge pulsed regularly, a dirty scum of foam spreading in a wide periphery from the ship's side as the water from the flooded hold was returned to its natural element.

It wouldn't be long now. Before we would find out . . .

I flicked my cigarette in a wide arc towards the water and turned away. There wasn't any hurry to go back just yet. Barney would let me know if anything went wrong, and even if it did there wasn't much I could do about it now. While there was always that slim hope that I might still find a trace of John Templeton's last moments aboard.

Even the internal alleyways of the officers' accommodation

seemed drained of life, like the useless artery of a silent corpse. I shivered despite the warmth. Oh, there were all the sounds of a ship there, with the throb of the generators and the soft whine of the engine room fans from further aft. But there was something else too, something I thought had perhaps gone along with Lenz and the Menteses – because there was still an indefinable, suffocating atmosphere of . . . menace?

The ship rolled, rising quicker to the swells as she slowly regained her buoyancy forward. Then she heaved again, only a hardly detectable jolt, but it told me the seas were already starting to build once more as the new gale gave them life far away to the north west.

I hoped the patch would hold. Just to spite the bitch!

A door banged incessantly, swinging on its hinges with every sway of the accommodation. Absently I stopped outside and reached for the handle, intending to shut it. Then I noticed the printed white sign against the varnished teak facing – *Chief Officer*, with presumably the same legend inscribed in Turkish below it.

Curiously I glanced into Tilsley's cabin. He was still the complete enigma to me. An elegant Englishman holding a First Mate's berth aboard a Turkish ship. And a competent seaman too, as I'd observed during the past few days yet, at the same time, occasionally diffident and hesitant – like that time on the gale-lashed poop when *Tactician*'s rocket line fell across his shoulders.

And there was still that inconsistent impression I'd formed earlier. Of a man who was perfectly able to hold his own in any slanging match, yet still giving the appearance of being strangely apprehensive, almost nervous, in the company of his Bosun.

And of the open contempt Lenz seemed to hold for his senior officer. And the way Tilsley had been so cheerful, so relieved, when *Tactician* had finally sailed with Lenz and the Menteses aboard . . .

I stepped across the coaming and looked around. The cabin

was as tidy as Tilsley always seemed to be, though I'd noticed that he'd given up wearing that immaculate doe-skin reefer for the moment. Maybe Mike Tilsley had suddenly found that it was what you did that mattered, and that to show pride in being First Mate of a ship which had killed most of its crewmen wasn't the most endearing way of commanding respect.

A photograph on the bunk shelf caught my eye. I bent down and looked at it curiously. It showed a group of Royal Naval officers in one of those inevitable Victorian-style, tallest-at-the-back shortest-at-the-front groups they insist you pose for at the end of every RN specialist course.

Third from the left in the rear rank was a much younger, embarrassed-looking Tilsley. The single sub-lieutenant's ring on his battledress seemed very new, even in such a small scale image. I examined the other faces in the picture closely but none of them were familiar — maybe I was still subconsciously trying to find some connection between Tilsley's past and the *Sarikamis*'s present.

The neatly written label on the mount said H.M.S. VERNON. OCTOBER 1954 . . . Thoughtfully I straightened my back. Another little warning bell was tinkling in my mind but I shrugged it off. Tilsley's unusual background was becoming an obsession now, and quite possibly blinding me to the real, current mystery which still enveloped the *Sarikamis*.

I glanced quickly into the small bathroom which led off the Chief Officer's sleeping cabin. A roughly bundled pile of clothes had been thrown in one corner and I couldn't help grinning a bit when I saw it was that once pristine reefer Tilsley had worn when we first met him. Only now it was soiled and oil-stained, and even the braid on one sleeve had been partly torn away. It appeared that our sartorial First Mate was learning about the less glamorous side of the salvage business the hard way.

But this wasn't finding John. And I was beginning, despite my misery, to feel a professional interest in how things were going with the flooded hold again. Maybe it was still in my blood, the salvage game. Or was it my irresistible urge to keep on tilting at that old adversary, the Dragon?

I headed for the door, then hesitated, starting to feel a bit irritated with myself at taking even this illicit peep into another man's secret things. But there was an airmail letter lying on the writing desk and the postmark stirred a chord in my memory . . . *Marseilles*!

And then I did remember – Marseilles had been the *Sarikamis*'s last port of call before she headed west. And then swung south to steam towards Ras oum Achiche. It had been the last place she'd visited before Lenz – either with or without Captain Koroglu's blessing – had tried to destroy her.

Feeling even more guilty I picked the envelope up. It was addressed to Tilsley, c/o Messrs Hazar, Melen & Company, Ankara. I noticed the date on the postmark was six weeks old, which suggested that the *Sarikamis*'s Chief Officer would have received it before the ship sailed from her home port. And before they called at Marseilles for the last time.

I muttered, 'Oh bugger it!' and withdrew the thin blue sheets of paper, unfolding them carefully and glancing at the last one first to see who'd written it.

It was signed *Ronnie . . . Your affectionate brother, Ronnie*.

I did replace it then, without reading it. But even while doing that a single phrase attracted my eye, almost at the bottom of that page. It said simply, '. . . give Dad's present to the skipper of the pilot launch. He's agreed to the proposition and knows where to bring it, so it's okay for this trip.'

I didn't read any more. It's not right to probe too closely into confidential family business. But I couldn't help wondering what kind of present Tilsley's Dad had, by now, presumably received . . . because pilot launches usually arrive alongside an inward-bound ship first.

Before even the Customs do.

But that was strictly Tilsley's business. And Ronnie's.

So I slipped the letter back into the envelope, replaced it carefully on the desk, turned towards the door . . .

. . . and came face to face with Chief Officer Michael Tilsley!

Who was watching me. Very, very closely indeed.

I felt the flush of embarrassed guilt burning at the roots of my hair. This was one time when Tilsley really would be entitled to haul off at me while all I could do was to keep my mouth shut and take it. And I was certain he would – some uneasy sense told me he'd been standing at that open door for quite a long time. Almost as long as it takes to open up a strictly private letter and read it.

Only all he said was, 'Looking for me, Captain?'

Quite mildly. Even a bit pleased, in a way.

I blinked at him and swallowed. 'Yeah . . . ? Oh, yeah. I wondered . . . that photograph actually. It sort of caught my eye when I glanced in.'

He grinned. It was the first time I'd seen him genuinely amused and he looked a completely different person. Much nicer. He nodded towards it. 'Portrait of a very young sea dog. Still being sent for buckets of steam and green oil for the starboard lamp.'

I made an effort to gather my wits. 'You were in the RN then. Obviously.'

'Early fifties. National Service. Though I'd thought about making a career of it . . . until their Lords of the Admiralty decided that commerce was my true vocation, so I went deep sea with the Merchant Navy.'

'The *Turkish* Merchant Navy?'

He shrugged. 'My father. Used to be in shipping in the UK. Then Hazar, Melen offered him a superintendent's job and I went with him . . .' The Mate hesitated. '. . . it seemed a pretty good idea. At the time.'

'But?'

'Oh nothing . . .' He looked at his watch and then at me. 'Look, d'you mind if I ask a favour?'

I heard someone running along the boat deck outside, then turning into the officers' accommodation. I hoped they were looking for me. I just couldn't get rid of that bloody awkward feeling of embarrassment. I said, 'Sure. What is it?'

'I'd like to borrow one of your inflatables for half an hour. Take a run ashore in the sun. While we're waiting.'

I spread my hands, still half listening to the noises off 'Yeah, why not. It'll be a bit longer yet until we know about the patch.'

Then Barney arrived at the door looking worried. 'Skipper? We've got a snag. One of the pump intakes is blocked by something in the hold. Mike's going down to look but I thought you'd like to know.'

Tilsley grinned at us. 'This I'll leave to the experts . . . I'll bring you some seashells back.'

I followed Barney through the door, then turned back to Tilsley. Something about that photograph still niggled me but I couldn't quite place it. I half opened my mouth to ask him what he'd done in the Navy then Barney called anxiously, 'Skipper?'

So I just said, 'A tall, cold beer'd be better than those shells of yours. Don't stay away too long.'

And followed the Second Mate towards the still flooded forward hold.

The water level had dropped about eight feet since I'd left, which suggested that the patch was holding up pretty well against the outside pressure. The water itself looked even dirtier, with that slowly revolving scum and the tops of sodden bales of mohair projecting like contaminated, fuzzy islands from an ink lake.

They'd stopped both pumps temporarily, in case the suction from the still clear strainer trapped the man diving to examine the other. As I watched, Mike's head broke surface and I felt again that tremendous respect for those divers, working often in pitch dark, impenetrable conditions with only their sense of touch to help them. It was similar to a surgeon operating in a blacked-out theatre, wearing a mask and a blindfold.

And while they were doing it, breathing canned air through a vulnerable plastic tube.

Mike spat and called cheerfully, 'I've found the intake. There's something soft against it — probably a bale of mohair — so send a line down an' I'll make it fast.'

One of the riggers allowed a rope to uncoil into the hold. Mike grabbed it, then his head disappeared again and the line followed like a nylon trace taken by a salmon. I glanced around the square of the hatch and saw the salvage crew all leaning over, watching anxiously, and wondered what was really driving them to do this lousy job anyway.

Or maybe every last one of us had his own personal Dragon. In some form or another.

Mike seemed to be down there for a very long time. I noticed the men looking at each other queryingly while, beside me, Barney started to shuffle anxiously. Then, abruptly, the head broke water once again and Tracey tore off his mask, inhaling heavily in long, rasping gulps of air.

And, this time, he looked white and strained.

'Haul away . . . *gently.*'

Someone called jokingly, 'Bloody divers. Bit of a swim, give a few orders, an' us poor bastards have to do all the wor . . .'

Mike Tracey yelled tightly, 'Jus' haul AWAY! And gently, for God's sake!'

I felt, rather than saw, Barney gazing at me questioningly. He'd noticed too — we all had, judging by the hush that fell over the crowd around the hatch. But Mike Tracey's voice had an edge to it which verged on barely-controlled hysteria.

An icy-cold, prickling ghoul started to stroke the nape of my neck with anticipatory fingers.

Slowly the rigger took in the slack on the line. It went taut and he pulled harder but it still wouldn't budge, then the man next to him silently took the tail of the rope and gradually they retrieved the sodden weight which had been blocking the pump intake.

Until, without any warning, it broke surface.

And the men around the square of that hatch gave a long, explosive sigh of horror . . . !

The hand of the Thing came first. And then the arm, with the bright orange line secured tightly around it. And then the head, all hanging to one side and lolling hideously to prove the neck was broken. And then the rest of It – rising in jerky, bouncing twirls with the aerated, noxious water streaming down in a twinkling cascade reflecting the sun above.

And then they had eased the poor swollen corpse over the coaming and laid it ever so gently down on the warm steel deck. I felt my legs carrying me hypnotically towards it, pushing through the staring, silent men, while all the time my mind kept screaming, 'No! Please God don't make me look at it . . . Not actually *at* it, God . . .'

Until I was there beside it. And the salvage men moved back and stood gazing at the deck, nervous hands fumbling with doffed caps as each and every one of them shuffled like Sunday School children suddenly seeing an elder's grief.

It wasn't Johnny's face any more yet, at the same time, I knew that it was. Because now I was gazing at that very same image which had floated in and out of the yellow-green weed around the sunken patch, when I'd dived the previous days. An inhuman, bloated mask staring up into the sun with blank eyes, just as my fevered imagination had conjured forth while I swam under the hull of the stranded ship.

Only in that instance it hadn't been real – because John Templeton had been aboard the *Sarikamis* all the time.

Barney whispered, so low I could hardly hear him. 'There's something in its . . . in his hand, Skipper.'

In a daze I knelt unsteadily beside the corpse and ever so carefully eased the bleached white fingers of the right hand apart. Something glinted as the sodden scrap fell to the deck and lay there, a final condemnatory message from a dead friend.

I started running. Cleaving a berserk path through knots of shocked, uncomprehending men.

Because for the first time I suddenly knew, beyond any doubt, who really *had* wrecked the *Sarikamis*.

John had just told me . . .

. . . when he gave me that scrap of cloth from a man's sleeve. With the three gold rings of a Chief Officer still adhering to it!

CHAPTER TWELVE

Tilsley was still struggling with the big Mercury over the transom of the inflatable when I caught up with him. He saw me before I'd got even half way down the accommodation ladder, but I think he had been expecting me – had known I would come after him.

He looked up and smiled softly, a bit ruefully. 'I never could start a bloody outboard motor anyway.'

And then he pointed the gun at me. It was an awfully big gun. And suddenly I was very frightened as well as being full of hate and anger. But not suicidal anger – that wouldn't help to avenge John's death one bit, while the *Sarikamis* . . . ? Oh, she would only give a great, booming laugh as the seas finally broke over her, and then she'd die as well. Like she'd always wanted to, ever since I'd first seen her.

And I couldn't allow her the pleasure of doing that. Not now.

So I just snarled bitterly, 'It was you, wasn't it, Tilsley? You and Burak together – John Templeton, McKay, Koroglu . . . all those poor bloody Turkish shipmates of yours . . .'

He shook his head. 'Not the *Sarikamis* crew, Ross. That was an accident. Burak lost his head, gave the order to abandon. The men thought it had come from the Captain . . . and I couldn't halt the panic.'

'Why not? Because you were too busy sabotaging the falls of the Captain's boat?'

Tilsley smiled again, but the rueful air was fading. '*Touché!* I suppose you could debit some of those deaths to my account, at that. But I had to make sure Koroglu died. He was the only man aboard who did know what happened up there on the bridge, just before we altered course away from the cliffs.'

I felt the ship lean over towards us as the biggest roller yet came in from the sea. Another few hours and the weather could really break – not that it would matter all that much, the way things were going right then. Tilsley felt it too and stepped carefully out of the inflatable, back on to the bottom of the ladder. But the barrel of the gun didn't waver one inch.

'So that part of your story was the truth then – the Captain actually did attack you on the bridge. Only *he* surprised *you*. He threw the auto-pilot off course . . . and then what? Did you kill him at that time?'

'He was an old man, Ross. I didn't hit him back very hard.'

'No? Like you didn't try an' run *Tactician* down very hard, either.'

He shrugged. 'Spur of the moment decision. I didn't know then why you were waiting there so conveniently . . . But I always said that involving Burak was a big mistake. He was too nervous, far too risky for our kind of business.'

I snapped quickly, 'Said to whom, Tilsley . . . ? And exactly what *is* your kind of business anyway? Apart from killing people?'

Only this time he didn't answer. He just stole a wary glance at his watch and it reminded me of the way he'd kept looking at it after he'd surprised me in his cabin. A whole twenty minutes ago. An eternity.

But why? He must have known there wasn't any pressing urgency to leave. This part of the ship was deserted, the rest of the crew still muttering in shocked groups on the forward deck, and the very fact that I was alone must have told him I was still the only man aboard who knew enough to put three gold rings together, add them to all the other bits and pieces, and come up with four.

Yet there was something else about him too. That air of suppressed urgency mixed, at the same time, with a curious hesitancy. A reluctance to terminate the conversation – presumably with a full stop. Made by a bullet.

It was almost as though he felt compelled to keep on talking, to reveal the full story of the *Sarikamis*. Perhaps it was understandable, in a way – every man has to share his guilt with someone. Or maybe Tilsley was just an extroverted killer who needed to prove how clever he'd been.

Just before he killed the confessor as well.

I tried again, desperately. Anything to delay his pulling that trigger. 'All right then. But where do Lenz and the Menteses fit in?'

He frowned and looked genuinely puzzled. 'I don't know, Ross. I honestly don't know about them at all.'

I stared at him, feeling ridiculously outraged. Lenz and the other two had undoubtedly murdered Burak with cold-blooded deliberation – which suggested they were somewhat more than just ordinary, happy-go-lucky sailormen for a start. And then there were all the other more indefinable things . . . like the way Lenz had treated Tilsley with that almost open contempt. As if he knew quite a lot more about his Chief Officer than was shown in his seaman's discharge book.

Yet Tilsley was pretending not to understand? In other words he was expecting me to believe that the *Sarikamis* had carried not one, but *two* entirely unconnected groups of killers . . . ?

I forgot about the gun and snapped aggrievedly. 'Oh, come off it, Tilsley. Now pull the other one.'

He seemed quite upset that I should doubt his words, but I couldn't help remembering what an actor he'd now proved to be. Like that time back at the very start, when we'd stood gazing at a beach full of drowned corpses, and Tilsley had looked so very British and sad but with just the right amount of stiff upper lip.

Only this time I knew somehow, that he really was telling the truth when he repeated, 'I honestly don't know, Ross. As far as I'm concerned Lenz and the Mentese Brothers are ordinary crewmen . . . and the only reason they didn't abandon with the rest was, presumably, as they told you – that they were trapped until the boats had left.'

But I could see it was worrying him, too. Probably a lot more than me, in a way.

So it was my turn to shake my head. I'd been trying to console myself with the thought that, at least, when I died I'd know precisely why – only now I was even more confused than ever, and the mystery of the *Sarikamis* had become more and more incomprehensible.

Two separate groups of homicidal maniacs plotting individually aboard the same ship? Plotting and counter-plotting. One lets anchors go, the other secures 'em again. One saws through wire ropes, the other re-rigs them . . .

. . . Jesus!

It was almost the classic black comedy situation – except that seventy-odd dead men weren't laughing.

I saw the gun start to twist as Tilsley's grip tightened on the trigger. I know my voice revealed the hysteria within me but I didn't give a damn. I just had to stop him killing me.

'*Wait*, Tilsley. Please. One more question . . .'

He seemed to frown disappointedly for a moment, then the grip on the gun relaxed fractionally. I had to take a chance, a gamble on the kind of man he really was, so I tried to control my fear and quite deliberately played my last card.

And hoped he was as conceited as he was cold-blooded.

'You're one man, Tilsley. All alone apart from a nervous kid. Yet you've apparently done exactly as you planned all along. Maybe just with guts and sheer determination . . .'

'Thanks for the approval, Ross. Now the question, huh?'

But he looked a bit pleased, all the same. And secretly proud. I think it was then that I realised Michael Tilsley was a little mad. But only mad in a special kind of way – and that could just make him a tiny bit more vulnerable.

I took a deep breath and shook my head mockingly.

'Approval? Oh no, Tilsley, nobody earns approbation until it can be measured against the original task. Don't expect me or anyone else to clap when we don't even know what it was that you set out to do in the first place.'

He didn't look quite so pleased. 'I've done precisely what I intended ... or will have. Quite shortly.'

That last remark put the first seed of an unpleasant thought in my mind, but right then it seemed a question of priorities. I grinned nastily and shrugged.

'So everyone gets lucky occasionally. You don't need brains and guts, not if you've got luck on your side.'

The petulant irritation on Tilsley's features told me that I was still very close to death – until, quite abruptly, he started to smile like a secretive little boy after a successful raid on the jam pot and I realised, with a faint sense of revulsion, that all of a sudden we were playing a game. A ghoulish, perverted kind of game which I myself had invented.

And which I was about to play.

'All right, Ross. Get back up that ladder,' he grinned. 'I'm going to show you something. And prove to you that the only one who needs that luck of yours is you. And your salvage crew.'

A breaking sea slapped the bottom of the ladder, bursting in a haze of fine spray. I hoped Tilsley would be caught off balance but he just jerked the barrel of the gun peremptorily and said, 'Up! Or I can shoot you now if you'd prefer it, of course.'

I started to move. Tilsley had an even better approach than Tanker towards getting a man to do what he wanted ... and that made me think about Tanker again. And that distant ship to seaward that I'd seen from the boat deck earlier, when I'd wondered if it could be *Tactician* returning from Djidjelli. Only I wasn't able to see it now anyway, because the bulk of the *Sarikamis* was between us and whatever it was.

Either way it wouldn't be good strategy to warn the man behind me ...

I halted at the top of the ladder. The centrecastle accommodation was still between us and anything approaching from the sea. Glancing quickly forward I prayed desperately that someone would be looking this way, but the upper decks were deserted. Barney and the rest of my crew were still masked by the break of the well deck, presumably waiting uncomfortably around the body of a drowned man for me to return after my apparently inexplicable flight.

'Skipper's flipped his lid, poor bastard . . . Mind you, they was real mates, him an' Mister Templeton there . . . Aw, leave him alone a bit, Barney. Let 'im get over the shock . . .'

So nobody would come looking for me. Not for a while yet. Until it was too late.

'Where to now, Tilsley?'

He stepped off the ladder as well, watching me very carefully with that secretive, pleased sort of smile still on his face. I still didn't dare let my eyes wander towards the forward corner of the alleyway to see if *Tactician* was out there so I just moved cautiously to one side to hold his attention, prevent him from glancing casually out to sea.

Only now I couldn't tell whether Tanker was out there with the tug either.

Not that the Bosun would be able to do all that much anyway – apart from look surprised when Tilsley shot him as well. Dammit, Tanker was just a salvage hand. He didn't even own a gun . . . or I didn't *think* he owned a gun . . .

Because, for that matter, I wasn't so sure whose side Tanker was on. And come to that, wasn't it just possible that Tilsley's apparent obsession with time could even have something to do with *Tactician*'s return . . . ?

Then the *Sarikamis*'s Chief Officer looked at his watch yet again and the uneasy feeling over that earlier remark of his returned even more forcibly – when he'd said, 'I've done precisely what I intended . . . *or will have. Quite shortly.*'

And then the apprehension snarled into a tight, sick knot in my stomach.

As I noticed, for the first time, the varnish of nervous sweat across his forehead, and that mixture of tension and barely suppressed excitement. The kind you'd expect to see on the face of a very special kind of gambler. A gambler who played almost against his will.

A gambler playing a game called 'Russian Roulette.'

Just before Tilsley smiled challengingly, but only with his lips. Then said, 'We go aft, Ross. To number six 'tween deck . . . where the mines are stowed.'

It seemed a very long climb down to the lower 'tween deck in number six hold. But most of that cargo had already been unloaded at the previous port of call – Marseilles.

Where Ronnie lived. Who wrote letters.

And Dad. Who apparently had his presents smuggled in care of the local pilot launch . . .

I did hope he'd had a happy birthday. He deserved one. As a consolation prize. Because he'd made such a lousy job of being a father!

Son Number Two dropped lightly from the last few rungs of the ladder and stood in the square of the hatch behind me. A shaft of sunlight carved through the shadows and silhouetted him against a silvery haze of swimming dust particles. He looked just like a saint in the stained glass windows of a church.

Except for the gun.

Which he jerked towards the other side of the hold. 'Over there, Ross. You'll find a light switch behind that after pillar.'

I was glad of that. I didn't want to be shot in the wrong place, when I did get shot, and with only the small corner of canvas turned back there wasn't really enough light to guarantee a quick kill. And maybe those bloody mines would look just a little less menacing in the naked glare of the cargo lamps anyway.

I noticed, as I crossed the hold, how the ray of sun from above slowly moved across and back, across and back. Like a theatre spotlight on a darkened stage. Only this spotlight told me that the *Sarikamis* was rolling more and more as those seas from the north west swamped into the bay. But I didn't think that would matter very much. Not now.

So I switched the lamps on. And stopped dead.

Because sitting there, right in front of me, was my one very special sea mine — the one with the tadpole-painted personality. Just as it had done on that horror-filled night before Burak was hunted to his death, and John Templeton had disappeared.

But *was* it quite the same? Or was there something just a little different about it now . . . ?

Though right then it wasn't that particular mine which was frightening me so much as what lay beside it, where its brother sphere had originally taken up the other position in the rank.

Because now my exclusively marked tadpole mine was nestled against a very empty space.

While its adjacent, common-or-garden contact mine, which had been there on my last nocturnal visit, had . . . well . . . disappeared.

Maybe it was the shock of it. Or just the fact that I'd had an abrupt reminder of the one real threat which still hung over the stranded ship. But all of a sudden I remembered a picture — and at least one small part of the *Sarikamis* jigsaw puzzle began to fit into place.

One hour too late . . .

'*Vernon*,' I whispered stupidly.

Tilsley's voice behind me sounded a bit disconcerted. 'Who?'

I swung round abruptly and the gun wavered nervously. But I was far too preoccupied with a photograph above a bunk, and the faint warning bell it had rung in my mind but which I'd ignored — when, all the time, I'd been gazing at the one positive clue to the riddle of the detonators stolen from the strong room.

And the one fact which indicated that they weren't taken

by Tanker after all. Only until now there hadn't been any other suspect we knew of who might understand the mechanism of a contact mine . . .

I said again, savagely, '*Vernon*, Tilsley. That photograph in your cabin shows you did part of your National Service training there. And H.M.S. *Vernon* is the Royal Navy's mine and torpedo school, dammit!'

He grinned at me with that pleased expression again. 'I said you don't need luck when you've got brains, Ross. And I found that the arming procedure for contact mines hasn't changed all that much, not even in twenty years.'

But the full import of what he was suggesting didn't really register for a moment. I was still trying to understand why the hell *Tanker* should have been so interested in those mines too, then. And how he could have known about those stolen detonators without our telling him . . . while I was also too bitter with myself for having had the one piece of evidence staring up at me which did tie Tilsley up with the theft – and consequently established his involvement in the whole lousy *Sarikamis* affair.

And at a time when we could have jumped him quite easily, Barney and I together. Long before he could have produced that gun . . .

Tilsley glanced upwards in an odd sort of way, and said proudly, 'I'm pretty good with blocks and tackles too, Ross.'

My eyes absently followed his, wondering irritably what was so bloody fascinating about twenty feet of empty hatch space high above our heads. I didn't need Tilsley's watch to tell me time was running out for Peter Ross, frustrated salvage man, and I hadn't even scratched the surface of the *Sarikamis* mystery yet. There was the bloated shadow of Karl Lenz, for instance. Now gone but still, somehow, a part of everything that had happened despite Tilsley's obvious reluctance to believe it.

Or *was* Lenz just a coincidental horror? Some sort of temporarily resting hood who'd killed Burak just to keep his hand in . . . ? Only that wouldn't explain the equally sinister involvement of the dark-skinned Brothers Mentese. Or their fanatical efforts to save the ship while Tilsley was trying so desperately to sink it.

And then there was the most inexplicable mystery of all. And that was why the *Sarikamis* had to be destroyed in the first place . . . ?

My wandering glance caught the glint of something high above. Something moving pendulously, regularly. As if swinging with each slow roll of the ship.

I froze. Rigid. While the whole world seemed to spin crazily around me.

Because – all of a sudden – I'd found that missing contact mine.

As Tilsley had said – he was pretty good with blocks and tackles.

It must have been quite an accomplishment, rigging that three-fold purchase and then, single-handed, heaving a dead weight of over a ton off the deck until it was suspended maybe fifteen feet above a man's head. And all that in the minimal light from a hand torch presumably – because he must have rigged it during the previous night and wouldn't have dared to risk the stray gleam of the hold lamps betraying him.

And now I knew where to find the stolen detonators too. Not that I wanted to look.

But what was the point? Admittedly the very sight of that huge, dangling Amatol-packed sphere was, in itself, enough to stop me breathing with the sheer terror of it – but it still couldn't be detonated surely? Not without one of those protruding, soft metal horns fracturing against an unyielding object . . . and even in that first, paralysed glance, I could see that the arc of its swing was far too short to allow it to make contact with the sides of the hatch square . . .

Tilsley's voice was little more than a barely-controlled

whisper. 'It's armed, Ross. And ready to blow!"

But I'd guessed *that* much already.

I dragged my eyes from the horror above. He was still staring upwards with such an expression of fascinated apprehension that I knew I'd been right about the Russian Roulette theory. Tilsley was a very screwed-up sailor altogether – not only did he lack even the most elementary trace of compassion and guilt, but he also got any kicks he was capable of through deliberately exposing himself to danger. Which would explain why he was that very special kind of lunatic who was prepared to risk his life to accomplish his ends.

Like driving an ocean-going freighter at full speed into a cliff face.

Or returning aboard with me when he could easily have killed me at the bottom of the gangway, and disappeared ashore before any of the others were aware of what was going on.

In fact the only flaw in that bit of amateur psycho-analysis was that, deadly as it appeared, Tilsley wasn't in any real danger. Because that mine still couldn't explode in a million years. Not unless someone hit it with a hammer . . . or the tackle which suspended it gave way and allowed it to fa . . .

I whispered numbly, 'Jesus . . . Oh dear *Jesus* Christ!'

As I finally detected, against the glare of the lamps, that one missing factor. The one element which proved beyond any doubt that – whatever his motives were – Michael Tilsley was utterly, recklessly mad.

But a genius, too. In a sick, perverted kind of way.

The mine was suspended from one of the hatch beams. Not an unusual thing in itself – every beam had several holes cut out of the steel plate for lightness, and they were a handy point to pass a wire strop through to provide a fixing point for the top pulley block of a temporary purchase.

Only it had to be very temporary. Those rough-cut holes had angular, unfinished edges which would chafe the strongest wire clean through in time.

But the Chief Officer of the *Sarikamis* had incorporated one minor modification to his particular arrangement. Because he'd replaced the conventional wire loop with ordinary, soft manilla rope.

Which meant that, with every slow roll of the ship, that rope chafed jerkily backwards and forwards against the rough metal edge of the cut-away section. And each roll sawed through another few fibres . . .

. . . until, inevitably, the dead weight of the mine overcame the steadily weakening manilla . . . and a half ton of high explosive plummeted vertically.

And a split second later quite a lot of those other one hundred and ninety-nine mines in the hold would be detonating in sympathy. As the *Sarikamis*, and the Scab Rocks, and a whole beach in Africa ceased to exist.

While the really sick twist – from Tilsley's warped point of view – was that nobody could be certain of just how soon it would happen. And that made it the perfect substitute for his kind of kick . . . where you put one bullet in a six-chambered gun, and then take turns at placing it against your temple. Before pulling the trigger.

This was Russian Roulette . . . giant family pack.

'You'll never get away with it, Tilsley . . .' I breathed, feeling all cold and dead inside. '. . . they'll hunt you down wherever you hide.'

He grinned at me like a living skull. I realised, with a sense of revulsion that he was even more frightened than I was . . . which, for him, must have been better than having the most beautiful woman in the world.

'No they won't, Ross. Because they won't even start *looking* for me . . .'

The sweat trickled freely into his eyes but he was too excited, too full of his own perverted ingenuity, to notice. '. . . because I'll be dead as well, don't you see? Atomised along with you and your crew in a tragic salvage accident.'

I stared at him. It was all so bloody brilliantly planned. And *I* thought *he* was mad . . . Yet in a very short time we would all be dead while he'd still be alive and well and living under a different name. Only I wouldn't die in an explosion, not like Barney and Mike Tracey and the rest, because Tilsley would shoot me before his nerve finally broke and he headed for freedom.

And judging by the way he seemed to be getting more and more flushed, I wouldn't have very long to wait. But, oddly, I didn't care much any more. Not for myself. Because the dream had gone with John, and I didn't think Tanker would ever forgive me for treating him the way I'd done. And the Dragon wouldn't really have won anyway. Not properly.

But the *Sarikamis* would have won, though. And by heaven but her dying would truly be a spectacle for the gods . . .

I said coldly, 'I still can't give you that approval, Tilsley. Not until I know what you were trying to do. And why you have to destroy this ship . . . why you *still* have to. Even though you could just shoot me and get away long before anyone can stop you.'

The ship rolled more sullenly and that horrible deadweight above us jarred sickeningly, taking a great, pendulous orbit like some giant child's elastic-tethered ball. The sweat was literally pouring down Tilsley's face now and I saw him flinch, staring upwards with that horrible, almost hypnotic expression. That icy cold veneer had finally started to crack — only he was too far away to surprise. I'd only die even earlier than scheduled, half way across the hold.

So I put every bit of contempt I could muster into my voice.

'Go on, Tilsley,' I jeered, hating him so much I didn't even need to pretend. 'Run away, laddie. Get out of it before it gets *really* close to dying time . . .

'Shut up, Ross!' he snarled. But all the time his eyes kept flickering back towards that bloody mine.

I shook my head and grinned savagely. 'No approbation,

Tilsley. No approval from anybody. In my book you're just a sick, gutless chancer who got lucky by accident . . .'

'Shut UP, Ross . . .' His voice rose to a near scream. '. . . Shut up, shut up, shut UP, SHUT *UP*!'

I watched the gun swinging on to my chest and I laughed out loud. '. . . a lucky lunatic, Tilsley. An' *gutless* . . . 'Cause you daren't even stay around long enough to tell me *WHY*!'

The shock of the sudden silence struck me almost like a physical blow. Only the creak of the ship, and the boom of the rising sea against the *Sarikamis*'s plates, and the whisper of a manilla rope slowly cutting the heart out of itself . . .

And then Tilsley seemed to sigh in a resigned, drained sort of way.

Before saying quietly, almost conversationally, 'All right, Ross! I'll show you why I have to make certain this ship never unloads her cargo . . .'

He smiled a little then. '. . . and perhaps we'll see how much courage you've got too, eh? You'll find a spanner and a sledge hammer behind the ladder. Pick them up. Very, very slowly!'

I frowned. 'I beg your pardon?'

It wasn't that I meant to be polite. I was just so surprised, both by the request and the utter normality of his manner. Though I shouldn't have been really – because this *was* the *Sarikamis*!

'I think you heard. Now, pick them up and take them over there.'

And, just for a moment, the barrel of the gun pointed to an old friend. I walked hesitantly over, carrying the tools, and looked at it nervously. It was my tadpole-painted mine.

The ship seemed to lift and roll all at the same time and there was a sharp *crack* from above. I swung round feeling the nerves at the corners of my mouth jumping frantically – to see Tilsley grinning openly at my shock this time, and looking so calm I wondered if he hadn't gone a little more mad, instead of less. Gone right over the brink where fear didn't exist in a man's mind any more.

'One strand gone, Ross. But there's still two more left. And you're *such* a brave chap anyway . . . D'you see the horns on that mine in front of you?'

Damn right I did. And there was something else about it too. Something different. That same feeling I'd had when I first came down with Tilsley struck me again — about this particular mine being not quite as I'd left it the night John died. But I couldn't identify it.

And the tadpole was still there, certainly. That same green-painted squiggle, just under the arming cover.

'What about them, Tilsley?'

'There are two lock nuts at the base of each horn, right? Securing it against the casing.'

'So?' I started to feel uncomfortable. Very uncomfortable.

'Unscrew the nuts, Ross. And remove them.'

There was a light rattling sound from above. Not the hanging mine this time. Maybe a piece of equipment on deck, rolling with the ship . . . I snapped tightly, 'Then what, Tilsley? After I've unscrewed the nuts?'

He was sweating again. I didn't think it was a very good sign, and uneasily I began to wonder if I had been right about those missing detonators after all — that they *were* in that orbiting do-it-yourself time-bomb up above. Or was Tilsley so utterly deranged that it had all been a horrific practical joke? And that the live mine really was one with a little green tadpo . . .

His eyes were hard, and the gun was very steady. 'And then you're going to hit the horn, Ross . . .

. . . with that sledge hammer.'

The nuts weren't very tight.

In fact the only reason I took so long to remove them was because my hands were shaking so much, and my palms so slippery with sweat, that I dropped the spanner twice — watching wildly as it skittered over the round of the mine casing to clang shockingly to the steel deck.

While Tilsley got such a sadistic boost from watching *my* fear for a change that he didn't even look up when another sliding, grating sound from above suggested a three-inch rope couldn't stand much more punishment.

He jerked the gun. 'Now pick up the hammer.'

I snarled angrily, 'Jus' *wait* a minute.'

Slowly I wiped the palms of my hands against the legs of my trousers. I was damned if I was going to give him one more moment of satisfaction. And if I got him rattled enough a second time there was always a chance he'd move in a bit closer.

But he just said, a little too mildly, 'I thought you wanted to find out why the *Sarikamis* has to blow, Ross?'

The hammer shaft felt smooth and cool in my hands. I wondered for the last time about just how insane Tilsley really was, and whether I would ever know the answer I wanted to find. Or was I about to be the triggering mechanism for two hundred sea mines?

Then I lifted the hammer.

Tilsley whispered, 'You're going to get quite a surprise, Ross . . .'

And he was quite right. Because I did.

Get a surprise, I mean. But without even moving a muscle.

Because an aggrieved voice from behind us growled, ' 'Course you never thought to suggest they might've had *guns*, did you?'

And both Tilsley and I pivoted with the shock of it.

To see Tanker and Lenz, and the smiling Brothers Mentese, standing watching us from the bottom of the ladder.

CHAPTER THIRTEEN

Tanker repeated petulantly, 'Well you *didn't*, did you . . . ? Tell me they might have had guns.'

I shook my head numbly. 'No. It never really struck me. Not about them having guns, anyway.'

He looked utterly disgusted with everything. 'Yeah, well it never struck those knot-heads on the foredeck either. Not 'til after they'd taken *Tactician*'s lines aboard. *And* made her fast alongside.'

It was unnerving, the way Lenz and the Brothers just stood there silently, watching us. It was bloody ridiculous too. Like having an irritable conversation about football – while you're waiting for a firing squad to take aim.

I said anxiously, 'The boys didn't try anything on, did they? When they found those three still aboard with you?'

Tanker stared pointedly at the weapons in the visitors' hands. Personally I'd always imagined cannons *that* big would've been on wheels. 'Are you kidding? Barney, Eddie Styles, Tracey . . . they're all locked up safe and sound in the bosun's store now.'

I felt a warm feeling of relief. But it didn't last. I had a pretty good idea that Lenz's appearance wasn't good news. Not for any of us. And certainly not for Tilsley.

I stole a quick glance at the *Sarikamis*'s Chief Officer. I don't think I've ever seen anybody looking so utterly lost. He just stood there, frozen to the spot, staring at Lenz, with a terrible, hypnotised incredulity and I didn't need any further proof than that to convince me that Tilsley was even more baffled than I was about the German's interest in the *Sarikamis*.

So why had Lenz hijacked *Tactician* – and then come all the way back here? What in God's name *was* so important about the *Sarikamis*?

I said, 'Johnny's dead, Tanker. Tilsley killed him.'

The understanding sadness in the Bosun's eyes told me that he already knew. And then the ship gave a bigger roll than ever, and I heard the mine tackle grate along the beam sickenly just as Lenz glanced curiously upwards.

I thought vicariously, 'Now it's *your* turn for a surprise, you big fat bastard!'

Only it wasn't quite like that. Because the pudding features ever so slowly wrinkled into lots of little folds and I realised, incredulously, that Karl Lenz was actually laughing instead. Standing underneath a mine, and bloody well laughing!

Just before he said, with great good humour, 'Presumably you are the so inventive man, Herr Tilsley. Even if a very foolish one also.'

I snapped recklessly, 'You'd better enjoy the joke, Lenz. That mine's armed and ready to blow the moment the strop gives way.'

The German shrugged and I knew that, whatever else he was, he didn't have a nerve in his gross body. 'There is still time for what I have to do, *Kapitan* Ross . . . But why did you remove the locking nuts from the other mine, hah?'

I jerked my head. 'Ask Tilsley. Nobody ever tells me anything.'

Slowly Lenz turned. He wasn't smiling any more. 'They said you would try to double-cross us, Tilsley.'

They? *They* . . . ? Who the hell are *They*? And *Us*, come to that . . . ? I started to get angry then. Resentful and bitter and terribly angry. Because I was going to die very shortly, yet eveeryone still insisted in talking in riddles. And the mystery hanging over the *Sarikamis* just kept getting deeper and deeper.

For the first time Tilsley seemed to come out of his trance. Only the unbelievable thing about it all was that *he* didn't appear to grasp what Lenz was talking about either.

'*Us*, Lenz? I don't kno . . . !'

The German nodded with sympathetic understanding. 'But you were not supposed to know, my friend . . .'

Quite slowly and deliberately he began to lower the barrel of the gun until it was aimed at Tilsley's knee cap. '. . . that you and I, and the excellent gentlemen Mentese, are . . . ah . . . business associates, hah? That all of us work for the same employer.'

Tilsley screamed, 'NO LENZ!'

Just before the roar from that huge weapon drowned even the crash of the seas against the *Sarikamis*'s hull.

The wind on my face seemed so wonderfully pure that, for a few moments, all I could do was to close my eyes and savour the cool fingers touching my skin.

And then I opened them again, and remembered I was still aboard a freighter called the *Sarikamis*, and that she could explode in a great, soaring ball of fire at any moment, so I stopped enjoying the wind and stared bitterly down towards the round, glistening black sphere which was now secured safely on the tug's after deck.

I couldn't make it out from the height of the *Sarikamis*'s well deck, but I knew there was a very special, wriggly mark under the arming cover of that particular mine. And I also knew that somehow, for some still inexplicable reason, that obscene cargo now transferred to *Tactician* held the whole key to the *Sarikamis* affair.

Only I didn't think I'd ever find the answers now. Because Karl Lenz was about to leave.

And I didn't think he intended to take us with him.

I remembered the look of utter horror on Tilsley's face, just before Lenz fired. Then the way he'd spun backwards to cling – still not really believing it could be happening to him – desperately to the ladder for support, with that ghastly, shattered leg trailing a pool of blood.

And I remembered the way Lenz had glanced up at the hanging time-bomb once again. And the way he'd nodded so approvingly at Tilsley.

And said sincerely, 'A most brilliant piece of ingenuity, Herr Tilsley. So inventive. And because of your enthusiasm I really do insist that you . . . ah . . . stay aboard. To watch the results!'

Then he fired a second time. While the Chief Officer of the *Sarikamis* collapsed in agony, not having a leg left to stand on.

But he'd got one thing he'd been after, even then.

Because somebody had finally appreciated his talent.

I remembered gazing at the writhing man with a terrible deadness inside me. And thinking about John, and McKay, and the kid who'd been swept over the side trying to re-secure a sabotaged rope . . .

. . . until Karl Lenz turned towards me, too, while I tensed myself for the third, and very personal shot. Only all he did was give a funny mocking bow before saying politely, 'I should be grateful for your assistance, *Kapitan* Ross. And that of your excellent Bosun. If you would be so good?'

And we were. Damn good. The way the silent Brothers Mentese were holding those guns suggested we ought to be.

So we removed the hatch covers from number six. Just like Lenz asked us to do. Only we didn't disturb that one steel beam which held the swaying mine . . . I don't think any of us imagined that would be a good idea.

We all ignored Tilsley, moaning softly below us.

And then Tanker and I swung the yardarm derrick outboard, right above *Tactician*'s after deck, and ever so carefully winched that other very special mine right up out of the hold and over the side. While, all the time, the horrifying product of Tilsley's twisted mind swung like a great black pendulum, ticking away the seconds that the *Sarikamis* had left . . .

. . . and I couldn't really concentrate because of the fascination that fraying length of manilla held for me. Sawing backwards and forwards, backwards and forwards . . . with the brown, fuzzy halo of the frayed strands getting bigger and bigger with every roll of the ship . . .

Actually, Tanker annoyed me a little at that part. Because he seemed to be more concerned with winching *Lenz*'s mine over to *Tactician* than he was with the one which was about to kill him. I remember seeing the look of utter concentration on his face as he swung it across the deck and outboard, before letting it down with a touch like the caress of a feather.

It reminded me of that time when we'd worked with the patch – when Rigger Garrity had died. And the concentration Tanker had put into that now somewhat irrelevant job. But he always had been a perfectionist. Even when it came to working for people who would congratulate him with a bullet in the head.

Vaguely I noticed the pumps were running again, too. Throbbing away on the foredeck where Barney had presumably re-started them all that time ago. After I'd left so abruptly in pursuit of Tilsley.

But the real irony of it all came when I finally realised – at that very moment – that we'd already virtually saved the *Sarikamis*. Because she was riding higher now, and lighter. Which meant the patch was holding and the pumps had nearly emptied the flooded hold which pinned her down to the Scab.

Only it didn't matter anymore. Because Lenz was going to let her blow herself up anyway. Just as soon as he'd gone, and that manilla couldn't hold its burden any longer.

But it *was* ironic. And I knew the Dragon would really appreciate the joke . . .

I turned wearily away from the rail and watched as Lenz came back aboard. He seemed very satisfied as he walked towards us. But he should have been, come to that – he'd got everything he came for, and now he was about to take it away first class. Along with *my* tug.

Or mine and John's.

They stood in a half circle around us. It made me think

179

of the way they'd closed in on Burak, just before they forced him to take a sixty foot step. Downwards.

I said tightly, 'Shoot and get it over with, damn you!'

Lenz stopped smiling and looked all hurt instead.

'I am not a cold-blooded killer, *Kapitan* Ross. Why should I shoot you?'

I stared at him. The most incredible thing was that he actually believed it.

'You mean you don't *want* us dead?'

He shrugged. 'It is not important to me either way. The radio equipment has been smashed, your rubber boats are sunk. We shall be a long way before you can warn the authorities . . . and I am a sporting man, *Kapitan*. I do not . . . what you say in England . . . pot a sitting duck, *ja*?'

I muttered '*Ja*,' numbly and looked at Tanker. He was watching Lenz in such a peculiar way that I began to wonder just how much he did know that I didn't. Which was most things. And then I saw the coil of fine wire in Lenz's pudgy hand and realised that, while he may have been a bit of a sportsman, he wasn't exactly going to leave us as evens favourites.

So they tied us both up, and as they did so I found that Karl Lenz was a much more accomplished sadist than Tilsley, because the way that wire bit into my wrists I knew I didn't have a hope of struggling free before the ship exploded.

They even propped us both against the hatch coaming. So we coud watch the pendulum over the pit. It was a refinement which Michael Tilsley would have been proud of . . . though at the moment he was lying underneath it, staring upwards through his agony, so I didn't think it would occur to him to think quite like that.

And then the Menteses had gone, preparing to get *Tactician* under way. Lenz examined the frayed sling with an expert eye and then came over to us for the last time.

'I will say "*Lebewohl*", gentlemen. Goodbye. You have, perhaps, twenty minutes left . . . We shall not meet again.'

I said, 'Let my crew go, Lenz. Take them with you f'r God's sake.'

He turned away. 'Twenty minutes, *Kapitan*. More or less.'

I was already struggling with the wire around my wrists as I stared at the squat, macabre figure which walked steadily away without even a backward glance. But I couldn't let him go like that, not without trying one last time to find something – anything I could – which might justify my dying.

I yelled, 'Lenz! I've got to know, Lenz . . . Why *did* Tilsley want to sink the *Sarikamis*?'

He seemed to hesitate for a moment, and then he turned towards me with a strange, almost a worried look on his face.

'You know, it may appear somewhat peculiar to you, Ross . . . but that is the one question I do *not* know the answer to myself.'

And then he was gone. And a few moments later the familiar throb of *Tactician*'s engine muttered steadily as she sheered away from the stranded ship.

While I exploded with all the pent-up hate and fear and misery in my soul. And bellowed an endless stream of obscenity which left me sick and breathless.

And every bit as ignorant as I'd been when the *Sarikamis* first headed at full speed towards the cliffs at Ras oum Achiche.

We sat like book-ends beside that open hold, Tanker and I. Back to back, and all the time I was venting my frustration I could feel his strong fingers bending the wire which bound my wrists, snapping it back and forth, back and forth to weaken it.

Like that bloody awful horror was doing to a thin strand of rope, less than twenty feet away from us.

And when I'd finally run out of breath, with my chest heaving like an exhausted bellows, he stopped working on the wire for a moment and sort of swivelled round until he was facing me, with an expression on his weatherbeaten features which was half admiration for my swearing technique, and half a look of genuine disbelief.

And then – with utter sincerity – he actually said to me, 'Christ, Skipper, but d'you really mean you don't know yet . . .

. . . why Tilsley an' Burak were trying to wreck this bloody ship?'

CHAPTER FOURTEEN

For a moment – for a very long moment – I stared at Tanker.

But I couldn't think of any way of killing him. Or not any quicker than Tilsley's mine would, anyway.

So I just said, very, very carefully indeed, 'Tanker . . . ? How can *you* possibly know why Tilsley and Burak wanted to sink this ship? When even Karl Lenz – who, I might add, had been involved all the way through – when even *he* . . . bloody well DOESN'T !'

He looked a bit upset, then he brightened. 'There's somethin' else I should maybe tell you firs . . . !'

The rope round the beam gave a crack like a pistol shot and I threw myself headlong across the deck. Then nothing else happened so I sort of half rolled back towards Tanker feeling a right idiot because, when that mine fell, there wouldn't be a lot to gain by being five feet further away from it.

It was still there. Only now I could see, with a chill of despair, that the second strand had gone. From now on that rope would only be one third of its original strength. And steadily weakening.

Tilsley's voice climbed up out of the hold, laden with all the agony of a broken human body. 'Help me, Ross . . . For God's sake, help meeeeee !'

But I remembered John's face again, when they'd lifted him out of the water. And the corpses bumping on that sun-drenched beach. And I decided Tilsley was in a pretty appropriate place anyway – right underneath that ghastly, one-ton brainstorm of his.

Tanker's fingers fumbled at the wire again. I couldn't see his expression now but the tone of his voice was as calm as ever. 'I was trying to tell you . . .'

I snarled, 'Shut up, Tanker. You just keep going at this bloody wire and I'll ask the questions. Right?'

He still persisted though. 'But all I'm . . .'

My voice must have been like a whiplash to him. But I knew we were dead men already, and I *had* to know.

'Shut your mouth, Bosun! And that's an order, by God . . . Now. Why – did – Tilsley – wreck – this – ship?'

He didn't answer for a moment, but the fingers worked at the wire. Then he said carefully, 'Aye, aye, Skipper . . . but can I tell it my way? Startin' with what Lenz said after he'd hi-jacked *Tactician*.'

The ship rolled gently, rising to the waves much quicker now. Now she was dry and almost afloat forward too. The mine took a great, arcing swing as well, and I hoped Tanker wouldn't be too long . . .

'Go ahead, Tanker,' I sighed wearily. 'But make it short. Please?'

And I just watched the mine below. And felt Tanker's warmth against my back. And listened to the answers to the riddles which had become an obsession with me. And turned a dream into an agony of salvage.

The real story behind the horror of the *Sarikamis* affair.

'Tilsley and Burak were crooks,' Tanker said. 'They worked for some international Syndicate . . . smuggling, mostly.'

'Lenz told you this?'

I felt him shrug. 'He was safe enough. He didn't intend our conversation to go any further . . . Anyway – this was Tilsley's biggest job. A half-million quids' worth of drugs, carried aboard this ship all the way from Ankara to the U.K. port of discharge – Liverpool.'

I whistled. Already I was beginning to understand what motive could lie behind the deaths of so many men. But not *why* they'd died. Not yet.

'How were they to be smuggled ashore? The drugs?'

'By the one certain, hundred-per-cent guaranteed way of

making sure H.M. Customs weren't goin' to poke around too enthusiastically . . .' He half turned and I could see he was grinning with a sort of half-jealous, half-grudging admiration. '. . . All packed inside the innards of a naval contact mine!'

I breathed softly, 'The tadpole . . . the little green tadpole.'

'You noticed that, then?' He sounded surprised. 'Yeah. And Tilsley's job, as Chief Officer, was to make quite sure that particular mine was discharged into a Royal Navy truck driven by some crook Jack Tar already primed by the Syndicate. Who would, presumably, go A.W.O.L. leaving one empty mine casing for Her Majesty to find.'

'Empty?'

'Your tadpole mine was a phoney, Skipper. Oh, the arming compartment was there, ready to take the det, the primer an' the battery. And the contact horns too, all ready to house the acid drops . . . but there wasn't no Amatol in it. No filling.'

'Just the drugs.' I stared out to sea, out across the line of the bulwarks and felt an unutterable sadness. I could see my ship, now. My ship and John's. Lying about half a mile off and, rather strangely, inshore of the Scab and stopped. But I didn't wonder why, not right then. There were too many other questions to answer first.

'How were they to remove them? At the British end of the line?'

'Through the locater holes for the horns. There are two nuts you unscrew, then . . .'

'Then you hit it. With a heavy hammer. To drive it inwards and leave a makeshift access hole in the casing . . .'

And I knew then that Tilsley really *had* been seeking my approval to bolster that perverted ego of his. And that he'd made me sweat all through a practical demonstration, down in that hold. Or nearly all through it . . . until Tanker and Lenz and The Brothers interrupted.

The mine over the drop gave another violent *crack* and, from below, Tilsley started a high-pitched howling, like an animal. A lost, terrified animal. Like those Turkish sailors must have howled as their orange boats toppled over and buried them.

I said urgently, 'But what about Lenz? And the Menteses?'

'Syndicate hoods. Sent to watch the watchers. Which is why Tilsley didn't know about them. A sort of insurance policy for the Syndicate. In case Tilsley and Burak tried to double-cross them and keep the drugs for themselves . . .'

And suddenly I knew at long last, without any more doubts, exactly why John and the others had died. And why Lenz had looked so worried and uncertain when I'd asked why Tilsley had wanted to wreck the *Sarikamis* . . . the one thing he really couldn't understand himself.

But *I* did.

Because I remembered a letter . . .

I felt the wire suddenly come a bit looser around my wrists but I didn't even try and prise them apart for a moment. And there wasn't a lot of point in it anyway, because the rope was too far gone to last more than another few seconds . . .

I snapped, 'Then they made a bloody awful job of it. Watching Tilsley. 'Cause he still got the stuff ashore, right under their very noses. In Marseilles.'

This time Tanker's voice sounded really surprised. 'How d'you know that? You said you din't know anything.'

I tugged frantically at the wires and then relaxed. They were still all snarled round and cutting into my flesh. 'A postmark. A phrase in a letter. The *Sarikamis*'s last port of call . . . it all adds up. Now.'

So I'd actually had it all. Staring me in the face. Long before Tilsley could ever have got away with it . . . I swung round violently, glaring suspiciously. 'But how the hell did *you* know the stuff had already been smuggled ashore? You never saw any letter in Tilsley's cabin.'

He was grinning at me and, just for a moment, I wished to God he'd start looking a bit more frightened seeing we were about to disintegrate in a mushroom cloud any second now.

'I looked. Inside the mine. I noticed that funny mark so I unscrewed the horns one night, an' found the casing was empty . . . mind you, I didn't twig what *had* been in it – not until Lenz started showing off aboard *Tactician*.'

'So Lenz and the Menteses still think they've got a mine worth half a million pounds aboard the tug . . .'

I started to laugh. It was all so bloody ironic. The whole of the *Sarikamis* affair . . . the plotting and counter plotting . . . My slowly crystallising suspicion of Tanker, when all he was doing was being as curious as me . . . except he did a better job because he was more familiar with those bloody terrifying horrors . . .

The wire went slack around my wrists and I started to move towards the hold like a crazy man. Like Tilsley. With the tears of hysteria coursing down my cheeks as I caught a glimpse of him below, crouched right under that pendulum of death with his shattered legs bent at right angles to his body like some hideous, deformed Indian beggar . . .

And I screamed down at him, 'I know, Tilsley . . . Now I *know* why you murdered all those helpless bloody sailors . . . an' wrecked this blood-soaked bitch of a ship . . .'

I started to shin out along the narrow beam, watching those last few strands inexorably prising apart and knowing, even as I clawed towards them, that I was far too late . . .

'You *had* to, didn't you, Tilsley . . . ? To save your own skin and Burak's . . .'

The ship gave a great, excited roll – almost as if she was already dead, and free to sail for ever over misty, supernatural seas.

'She had to be an unsalvable total loss, didn't she, Tilsley . . . ? because it was the only way you could prevent the Syndicate . . .'

I saw the mine gather momentum in a final, juggernauting arc which would snap the last few strands like threads. Right in front of my eyes.

So I just clung hopelessly to the beam, and jeered down at the mutilated animal below with all the sadistic hatred that only a man who'd lost a whole dream could ever muster . . .

'. . . prevent the Syndicate from finding you'd stolen their lousy cargo. 'Cause they'd've hunted you down and killed you wherever you hid otherwise, Tilsley . . . and now you're a dead man *anyway*, you poor . . . sick . . . cold-blooded bastaaaaaard!'

There was a *crack* like the snapping bones of a skeleton. I felt the fine strands of chafed manilla whipping across my distorted features . . .

. . . while the monstrous black-metal crustacean, trailing a tail of parted ends and spinning blocks, plummeted away from below me.

Right towards the bottom of the ship. And towards Tilsley!

I started to cry.

Because it was only a little explosion.

Hardly an explosion at all, really. More a sort of *crash*! The sort of noise you'd expect to hear when a detonator goes off.

Inside an empty mine casing . . .?

Ever so slowly I eased my screwed-up eyelids apart and stared down into the hold below. I could still see the mine – half a ton of it. Almost buried into the splintered hatch boards covering the lower hold.

I couldn't see a lot of Tilsley though. Not a lot. Because the rest of him was pulverised beneath the mine. Which was all very poetic, really.

So I sniffed a bit, and wiped my eyes with the tattered sleeve of my jersey, then carefully wiggled backwards until I reached the deck. And Tanker.

He looked at me a bit apprehensively. I suppose he didn't feel too secure right then, what with his hands still being wired behind his back and everything. And the expression on my face.

He said petulantly, 'I did *try* an' tell you, remember? Three times I tried to tell you. But you was too bloody keen to give orders, wasn't you?'

Silently I stared forward, to where *Tactician* was anchored inshore of the Scab. I wondered absently why Lenz had gone in there but, instead, I just said ominously, 'How did you know a box of detonators had been stolen, Bosun . . . unless you'd been forward in the strong room to pinch a *second* set yourself?'

He shuffled guiltily. 'Yeah, well . . . I didn't want to bother you, did I? What with the salvage problems and that. And we all knew some of those five nutters were up to their tricks. I just wanted to keep one step ahead, sort of.'

'You're trying to tell me that you actually armed *another* mine? While Tilsley was planning to do exactly the same thing . . .'

He grinned a bit then. 'They're safe enough. As long as you're careful.'

I stared at him, starting to chill all over. 'So *both* of those mines in that front rank were armed, then? Both ready to explode . . . only Tilsley's one didn't, dammit. And he was insisting I hit the other one – the marked one – with a hamm . . .'

And then a very unpleasant thought came into my mind. The same thought which had struck me earlier – when I couldn't quite understand what was different about my tadpole-painted mine, down in the hold.

Only now I knew. More or less.

The weatherbeaten face in front of me wrinkled into a huge, unashamed grin. He nodded outboard, over towards *Tactician*. 'Lenz figured to get far enough away from here to be safe, then remove the drugs from their stowage an' scarper. Him and the Menteses. All supposedly killed too, and out of the Syndicate's clutches . . . Just like Tilsley had figured it . . .'

I growled nervously, 'Tanker, what *have* you done . . . ?'

He didn't seem to hear me. There was a very wistful look in his eye. 'Lenz should just about be ready to open *his* mine now . . .'

The explosion, when it came, seemed to lift *Tactician* high in the air. Then she started to disintegrate, almost in slow motion, while the roar of the cataclysm rolled across the white foam of the Scab towards us. And then the debris . . . the little bits and pieces of our ship . . . spreading upwards and outwards as she, and Lenz and the Brothers Mentese, all blew into a fine spray of fragments . . .

I felt the wave coming, like the *Tsunami* of many nights ago. Only this one was in reverse. From inshore and thundering in great, stained gouts of spray against the black fangs of the Scab . . . and then against the bows of the *Sarikamis* herself, bursting with stunning fury into high-flung, hanging columns of foam and cascading downwards across the forward decks . . .

And then it had passed, exhausted by its own fury, and the ship was rearing like a startled foal as she backed away from the shore . . .

I lifted my head tentatively from the deck where I'd tried to bury it. He was already getting to his feet, a bit unsteady because his hands were still bound.

'How did you manage to change those mines around, Tanker? And why . . . before you left?'

'I reckoned it wouldn't do no harm, Skipper. To let Tilsley, or anyone else, think they were going to sink this ship with a dummy charge. If that was what they had in mind.'

'But the explosive filling – the Amatol? How the hell did you change *that* over?'

He looked a bit pleased at that. But not in the way the late Chief Officer Tilsley had looked. 'I didn't, Skip. I jus' collected a pot of paint an' a little brush . . .'

I felt very tired.

'. . . and you changed the marks. Just like that. You just changed the bloody marks.'

Which meant I had been right for the very first time. When it had struck me that, once upon a time, my tadpole mine had been on the opposite side . . .

I turned away and gazed inshore. There was a spreading stain of oil inshore of the Scab Rock, but that was all. And then, even as I watched, I saw the bows of the *Sarikamis* start to swing. Slowly at first, then more and more lively as the excited waves took her round, propelled by the backwash from the reef.

Tanker said disbelievingly, 'She's afloat! She's actually afloat, Skip . . . ! The wave from *Tactician* . . . An' the salvage award. By God but we can get ourselves another tugboat . . .'

We watched in silence for a long time, until the *Sarikamis* — as if finally absolved from the horror which had shadowed her — swung docilely on her two stern anchors and pointed her patched, battered bows towards the open sea.

I said quietly, 'Go and let the crew out, Tanker. We've got a job . . . a salvage job . . . to finish.'

And then I just stood all alone, and thought about John. And wondered if that dream we'd had wasn't already too far away to ever recapture.

Until a fierce but very familiar Dragon beckoned enticingly from the distant horizon.

Then, at that moment, I knew I'd still find a little bit of our dream. Somewhere.

And that John would always be there too.

To share it with me.

Fontana Books

Fontana is best known as one of the leading paperback publishers of popular fiction and non-fiction. It also includes an outstanding, and expanding, section of books on history, natural history, religion and social sciences.

Most of the fiction authors need no introduction. They include Agatha Christie, Hammond Innes, Alistair MacLean, Catherine Gaskin, Victoria Holt and Lucy Walker. Desmond Bagley and Maureen Peters are among the relative newcomers.

The non-fiction list features a superb collection of animal books by such favourites as Gerald Durrell and Joy Adamson.

All Fontana books are available at your bookshop or newsagent; or can be ordered direct. Just fill in the form below and list the titles you want.

-- -- -- -- -- -- -- -- -- -- -- -- -- -- -- -- -- --

FONTANA BOOKS, Cash Sales Department, G.P.O. Box 29, Douglas, Isle of Man, British Isles. Please send purchase price, plus 6p per book. Customers outside the U.K. send purchase price, plus 7p per book. Cheque, postal or money order. No currency.

NAME (Block letters) _____

ADDRESS _____

_____

_____

While every effort is made to keep prices low, it is sometimes necessary to increase prices at short notice. Fontana Books reserve the right to show new retail prices on covers which may differ from those previously advertised in the text or elsewhere.